OPEN
ICE

OPEN ICE

David Trifunov

James Lorimer & Company Ltd., Publishers
Toronto

James Lorimer & Company Ltd., Publishers acknowledges funding support from
the Ontario Arts Council (OAC), an agency of the Government of Ontario.
We acknowledge the support of the Canada Council for the Arts, which
last year invested $153 million to bring the arts to Canadians throughout the
country. This project has been made possible in part by the Government of
Canada and with the support of Ontario Creates.

Cover design: Gwen North
Cover image: Shutterstock

9781459415362
eBook also available 9781459415355

Cataloguing data for the hardcover edition is available from Library and
Archives Canada.

Library and Archives Canada Cataloguing in Publication (Paperback)

Title: Open ice / David Trifunov.
Names: Trifunov, David, author.
Identifiers: Canadiana (print) 20200203401 | Canadiana (ebook) 2020020341X
| ISBN 9781459415348 (softcover) | ISBN 9781459415355 (EPUB)
Classification: LCC PS8639.R535 O64 2020 | DDC jC813/.6—dc23

Published by:
James Lorimer &
Company Ltd., Publishers
117 Peter Street, Suite 304
Toronto, ON, Canada
M5V 0M3
www.lorimer.ca

Distributed in Canada by:
Formac Lorimer Books
5502 Atlantic Street
Halifax, NS, Canada
B3H 1G4

Distributed in the US by:
Lerner Publisher Services
241 1st Ave. N.
Minneapolis, MN, USA
55401
www.lernerbooks.com

Printed and bound in Canada.
Manufactured by Friesens in Altona, MB in January 2021.
Job #272149

For Cassandra.

Contents

1 Team CAPTAIN

All Jill Kang could see was a giant, screaming eagle. It was headed straight for her.

The eagle was the logo on a North Vancouver Thunderbirds jersey. It looked like it was flying down to snatch her in its claws and take her back to its nest.

That's it, Jill thought, *I'm lunch for a Thunderbird.*

Jill was lunging forward for a loose puck. In that position she had to decide. She could slam on the brakes, bail out and hope the Thunderbirds defender would overskate the puck. Or she could grit her teeth and make a play.

She knew the second option would result in her getting crunched.

"Heads up!" someone yelled from the bench.

There, that settled it. Everyone on the bench could see she was about to crash into the bigger defender.

But Jill realized in that moment that she needed to go all-out. It was the last game of the playoffs. If her team won, the West Park Queens would bring home the first trophy since girls had started playing Bantam hockey in West Park.

Jill was the captain of the Queens. Her team, she decided, was more important.

She stretched out her stick one last time. She nudged the puck between the defender's skates and over the Thunderbirds' blue line.

The defender stopped suddenly, throwing a big rooster tail of ice and snow up into the air. Jill could not stop and the two players collided.

"*Ooomph*," was the only sound Jill could manage.

"Ohh!" was all she heard from her teammates on the bench.

It did not hurt as much as Jill had expected. It hurt even less when she looked up and saw her linemate Alyssa skating hard on a breakaway.

Jill stopped hurting altogether when the referee skated past her with his hand in the air. He was about to call a body-contact penalty on the Thunderbirds defender who crashed into Jill.

Maybe, though, the Queens would not need the power play.

"Go, Alyssa!" Jill shouted.

Alyssa was about to shoot when the puck hit a rut in the ice. It dribbled off the blade of her stick. Alyssa pulled the puck back from the goaltender and tried a desperate backhand shot as the goalie came out to challenge her.

Team Captain

Jill got to her knees just in time to see Alyssa's shot sail over the goalie's leg pad and into the net. Alyssa herself crashed into the goal at almost the same time.

The referee blasted his whistle and pointed to the net. His shout of "Goal!" set the Queens screaming from the bench.

Jill tried to hug all her teammates at once.

"What a pass, Jill," Coach Harrison shouted. "Great play!"

Jill turned to greet Alyssa and the three other girls skating toward the bench.

"That was awesome," Alyssa said. "I so thought you were going to get smashed, Jill."

"I totally got smashed," Jill said. "But I don't care. You scored!"

Jill glanced up at the scoreboard: Queens 1, Thunderbirds 0.

"Just one more period, and we've got this," Jill said to Alyssa on the bench.

"How did you know I was there?" Alyssa asked.

The truth was that Jill didn't know Alyssa was going to get the puck. What Jill did know was that she had missed an easy pass. If she had received the puck properly in the first place, she would have never been forced into that play. Not for the first time, Jill wondered why she had been named captain of the team. She'd been playing only a couple of seasons. And there were much stronger players on the team. Like her best friend Alyssa.

But Jill did not want to show she was disappointed in herself. So she decided to laugh.

"Oh, we've been friends for so long," Jill said. "I guess I can read your mind."

Alyssa laughed right back. "Oh, no, don't tell Jake that you can read my mind. He's my twin. He's the only one I'm supposed to have a mental bond with."

Coach Harrison came up behind them and smacked their shoulder pads playfully. "We will call you the Crash Line from now on," she said. "Jilly crashes into the defence, and Alyssa into the goal."

Jill looked up and smiled. "I don't think I want to make a habit of crashing into people."

Alyssa laughed and nodded. "Yeah, shooting pucks into the net is way easier than sliding into it."

"Good plan," Coach Harrison said. "Take a breather. There's just two minutes left in the period."

Jill grabbed a water bottle from the bench. She squeezed a jet of water through the bars of her face mask into her mouth. She was still breathing heavily. The defender's knee had caught her just below the hip as she fell to the ice. *It will probably hurt in the morning*, she thought. But by then her team could be champions.

As Jill rubbed her leg through her hockey pants, the buzzer sounded to end the second period.

She walked carefully back to the dressing room, plopped down on the bench and took off her gloves and helmet. Then she stood and flexed her leg a few times.

"How you doing?" Alyssa asked.

"Fine. I'm fine," she said. "It'll be good. That's why we wear pads, right?"

She sat again and looked down at her leg. She wished she had newer pads instead of the second-hand gear her dad had bought at the equipment swap last year. The pads were starting to get thin, and Jill did not have one of those fancy girdles with extra pads to wear under her pants and socks.

"You two good to go?" Coach Harrison asked them.

"Oh, we are totally fine," Alyssa said. "No problems here."

Jill smiled, but she did not want to sit for too long. So she stood up, grabbed the bottle carrier and walked over to the sink to fill the bottles for the third period.

Standing definitely feels better than sitting, Jill thought. She put her helmet and gloves back on and led her teammates to the bench for the third period.

"One more period," Coach Harrison said as the referee called them to the ice for the faceoff. "Don't stop working. Don't stop believing in yourselves."

2 Penalty KILLS

The Thunderbirds were putting on pressure to tie the game as the clock ticked down in the third period. Jill kept telling herself that she wouldn't worry as long as the Queens were still leading 1–0.

Her next three shifts on the ice were unproductive. She didn't want to hurt the team, so she kept changing after only thirty seconds.

Coach Harrison gently tapped Jill's shoulder pads. "How's that leg, Jill? Do you want to go into the dressing room?"

"No, it's okay. But I don't want to hurt the team if I'm not playing my best."

Coach Harrison patted her shoulder pads again. She leaned close so only Jill could hear her.

"That's the kind of spirit that makes you a good captain. It's your choice," she said. "But don't worry about hurting the team. We're here to have fun together."

The coach moved down the bench and grabbed a cold pack from the first aid kit. She shuffled down the bench again and handed it to Jill. Jill slipped it under her hockey pants. The cold helped numb the leg right away. She looked up to the clock. There were still twelve minutes left in the game.

"We can do this, Queens!" Jill shouted.

Jill started feeling better, and it wasn't just her leg. She tossed the ice pack onto the ledge with the water bottles and got ready for her turn on the ice. She pushed her hand back into her glove as she stepped through the open gate.

She took a stride up the ice. She had to take advantage of the few minutes left in the game.

Heck, she realized, *it could be my last hockey game for a long time.*

"Alyssa, I'm open," Jill shouted to centre ice.

Her teammate dumped the puck on her wing, and Jill chased it to just outside the Thunderbirds' blue line. It suddenly felt familiar to Jill.

Just a period ago, this was where she had been caught in the collision.

She slammed on the brakes. That was all the Thunderbirds defender needed to get an advantage. The Thunderbirds collected the loose puck and skated back toward the Queens' goal.

"Don't shy away," Coach Harrison said as Jill returned to the bench. "You can do this. You are so much better now than at the beginning of the season. Go for it!"

Jill kept repeating Coach's words in her head as the teams traded chances.

"Five more minutes, girls," Jill shouted from the bench. "Dig deep!"

But just as she finished her cheer, the referee put his hand into the air and blew his whistle. He pointed to Leah, the Queens defender, and called her for tripping.

"Two minutes," the ref said to the bench.

"Don't worry about it," Coach Harrison shouted down the bench. "Let's kill this penalty. Who's next on the ice?"

Jill glanced at Coach Harrison, who smiled and shrugged her shoulders.

Jill took a seat in the middle of the bench. She wanted her strongest players on the ice, and that wasn't her. She tried cheering but could barely make a sound. "Okay, we can do this," she managed.

Jill looked up at the clock: two minutes, fifty-eight seconds to play. The faceoff was in the neutral zone.

"We got this," she called out, a little louder, as the referee dropped the puck.

Lily won the faceoff straight back to Maya, who skated back toward their net.

"She's such a good skater," Jill said to her coach.

Maya took the puck all the way around the net. Then, with two Thunderbirds closing in on her, Maya smashed the puck down the ice to kill some valuable time.

"Whoo!" Jill and her teammates cheered. The forwards came to the bench for a change. Coach Harrison banged Jill's shoulder pads, a little harder than Jill expected.

"C'mon, Captain," the coach said. "You can help us win this."

Jill dumped the ice pack back onto the ledge and stepped through the gate.

Her heart was pounding and her breathing was quick. She could feel the air rushing through her helmet. She glided to centre ice.

The Thunderbirds tried a long pass up the middle. Jill reached into the path and deflected the puck back into a corner of the Thunderbirds' zone.

She could hear her teammates screaming their approval from the bench. It gave her the confidence to keep moving. She pressured the defender, who had to send the puck across the ice to a teammate.

The only thing the Thunderbirds could do was dump the puck into the Queens' zone. Maya was there to collect it and shoot it hard back down the ice.

Jill looked up at the clock just in time to see it count down: *Three, two, one.*

All Jill could remember after that was her team throwing their gloves in the air and screaming around their goaltender.

Open Ice

★★★

The next thing Jill knew, she was sitting in the stands with Alyssa, a trophy in her lap. "We did it," she said softly to herself. "I can't believe we won!"

Jill was still staring at the trophy when Alyssa tapped her on the shoulder. "You listening?"

Jill looked up with a huge grin on her face. "No," she admitted. "Oh, your brother's game has started. It's already 1–0 for the other team? What happened?"

"Jake's team is probably going to lose this game," Alyssa said. "And then that's it for playoffs."

"That's too bad," Jill said. "Jacob is an amazing player." It made sense to Jill that Jacob was the captain of his team.

"Yeah, but the team is playing pretty badly. They were in first place for a while, but they haven't won for, like, a long time."

Jill was surprised to hear her friend talk that way. She had known the twins since kindergarten. Alyssa had always been her brother's biggest fan.

Jill was not sure winning mattered that much, anyway. But then she looked down at the trophy again.

Yeah, she thought. *It's pretty cool to win.*

3 Parkour Is WAY COOL

Jill slid into the back seat between Alyssa and Jacob. She held the trophy in her lap on the ride home. It was so tall she had to shift it side to side, depending on where she was looking.

"Thanks so much for driving me to all the games and stuff this year, Mr. Tate." She shifted the trophy toward Jacob to make eye contact with the driver through the rearview mirror.

"Hey, anything for the captain of the big winners," Alyssa's dad said as they pulled out of the arena parking lot.

"It was such a big help to my parents, you can't imagine," Jill said. "They were not going to let me play when they found out how much driving there was. They work weird hours. They told me to say thank you, and you're all invited to dinner next Sunday."

"Oh, yeah, we'll be there," Alyssa's dad said.

"Your mom can really cook," Alyssa's mom added.

"She learned from my grandmother," said Jill. "Nana lives with us, so she teaches me, too."

Alyssa's mom turned from the front seat with a big smile on her face. "Oh, that's a great idea," she said. "Alyssa, Jacob, we need to get you kids cooking meals, too."

Alyssa leaned forward. She grabbed the back of her mom's seat and smiled right back at her. "Oh, yeah? Who's going to teach us? Gramma's idea of cooking involves calling for reservations. Isn't that what she taught you?"

Everyone in the car shouted and laughed. Everyone but Jacob.

As Jacob shifted away to look out the window, Jill suddenly realized there had been tension in the car since they left the arena. She started to hum along to a song on the radio and Alyssa joined in. She pretended to play drums, too, until Jacob grunted uncomfortably in his seat again.

"Hey, Lys," Jacob said. "Can't you practice drums at home, alone, in your room? Maybe when I'm not around?"

Alyssa ignored her brother and kept right on swinging her hands in the air. She made some cymbal noises, too. "Pssh! Pssh!"

Jacob groaned again and mumbled something that Jill couldn't quite hear.

Seeing her brother was hating every minute of it,

Alyssa kept at it. Jacob grabbed the collar of his jacket and tried to pull it over his head, but he didn't even get close.

Alyssa burst out laughing. She was just about to raise her hands in the air for another burst on the drums when her dad interrupted. "Okay, little drummer girl, give it a rest. Give Jake some peace. His team wasn't as lucky as yours."

Once the car stopped outside Alyssa's house, Jacob bolted. Jill handed Alyssa the trophy so she could get out of the car.

"Not so fast, mister," Alyssa's dad called to Jacob. "Lug your gear from the back and air it out. And throw your stinky stuff in the wash, now."

"But Logan is on his way over," Jacob said. "I'll get the gear later."

"No way. It'll be next season before you realize it's been sitting in your bag all summer."

"What does it matter? I'm not playing next season."

Jacob grabbed his hockey bag and dragged it into the garage. Alyssa did the same.

"You sure you don't want us to drive you home, Jill?" offered Alyssa's dad.

Jill grabbed her gear and dropped it onto the driveway. *Clunk!* "No, don't worry about it," she said. "It's not heavy, and it's really not far. Plus, my bag has got these little wheels."

"Okay. Let us know if you change your mind."

Logan appeared from down the block. He clutched

a hockey stick with a plastic blade in one hand and held a bright orange street hockey ball in the other.

"You're not sick of hockey, Logan?" Alyssa's mom asked when she spotted him.

"Nah. Why?"

"Oh, well, Jacob tells us he's not playing next season. I thought maybe you needed a break after the season, too."

Logan looked over at his friend. "Huh? Three-on-three is starting, man. And you're moving up to Midget next season. Now is not the time to quit."

"I'm doing parkour instead," Jacob said.

Alyssa reappeared from the garage with a hockey stick of her own and a street hockey net. "I'm playing three-on-three, Logan," she said. "Don't worry about Mr. Grumpypants over there. He'll come around."

"Wait, wait," their mom said. "You two have got to figure this out. We can't swing two car trips in different directions. I thought we decided you both would play on the same three-on-three team. Do the new coed division, the fun one."

"Mom!" Alyssa and Jacob shouted together.

"That's the deal. I'm not driving you all over the city for another two months. You can join the coed team or you can both do gymnastics."

"Parkour!" Jacob shouted.

"Three-on-three hockey," Alyssa countered.

"That's the deal, take it or leave it."

Jill was amused by the brother-sister banter. But she was also curious. "What's the fun one?"

Alyssa placed the net on one side of the driveway and stole the hockey ball from Logan. Jill dragged her hockey bag to the grass and grabbed her stick. She tapped the blade on the pavement and Alyssa passed her the ball. Then Jill passed it back to her friend, who shot it into the net.

"We just found out about it. It's spring hockey," Alyssa said. "There's girls or boys teams, and a coed division. You should totally join. Dad said no at first, but there's this big tournament in Kelowna after the season. Dad remembered how much he loves wine, and how much wine they make there, so now we're going."

"Nice try at making it your dad's idea," Mrs. Tate said, cleaning out the front of the van. "But, yes, we'll sign you up if you and your brother join the same team."

Jill loved the idea of more hockey. She decided she would ask her parents that day. She collected the ball and passed it to Logan so she could grab her hockey bag and head home. He zipped a shot into the top corner. Jill jumped back as it whizzed past her.

"Yes, that's for the fans in Kelowna!" he shouted.

Jill laughed. But the more she thought about Kelowna, the more she wondered how she would afford a trip.

"Wait," she said. "We just finished playing. I'm not sure I can play another season *and* pay for a tournament."

Mrs. Tate handed Alyssa some empty water bottles as she made her way into the garage. "The season is short, so it doesn't cost that much, Jill. And, if it makes you feel any better, you're more than welcome to come with us to Kelowna. Logan is coming, so we'd need two hotel rooms, anyway."

"Yeah, I need you to come," Alyssa said. "Who am I going to talk to? My brother? No way!"

"It doesn't matter," Jacob said. "I'm done hockey. I'm doing parkour from now on. It's cooler, and there's no refs."

"Man, you're my captain," Logan said. "If you don't play, then who am I going to take orders from? Alyssa?"

"Oh, very funny," Alyssa said with a smirk.

Jacob looked at his friends, but didn't say anything. He picked up a hockey stick, rolled the ball around and shot it into the net.

"Yes! He's coming!" Logan said.

4 Just WARMING UP

Jill hauled her gear into the girls' dressing room of Vancouver Veterans Arena. She let her bag plunk onto the floor. Alyssa, who was following her, nearly tripped on it as she tried to find space on the bench near her friend.

"Oh, sorry. I didn't know you were so close." Jill was a little nervous.

Sitting on one side of the room were two of their Queens teammates, Lily and Macy. Across from them were two girls Jill didn't know.

"Hey, everyone," Jill said. She stashed her sticks in the corner of the room and went to say hello to the girls she didn't know.

"Hi, I'm Jillian, but my friends call me Jill or Jilly or Jilly Bean." The girls introduced themselves as Teagan and Camille. "It's really great to meet you both. Where did you play this season?"

"We were on Glenmore," Camille said.

"Oh, I remember your team. You had those cool

grizzly bear jerseys. What was your team again?"

Teagan was smiling.

"The Grizzlies," Camille said.

"Oh, ha! Of course." Jill knew she talked too much when she was nervous. She hoped these new girls wouldn't take it the wrong way.

The girls continued chatting as they dressed for their first game of three-on-three hockey. Jill was humming and talking to herself. "Where did I stash that tape? How many times do I need to dig through this thing today? Where is my mind?"

"You okay?" Alyssa asked her.

Jill looked up. "Huh?"

"You're talking to yourself."

"Oh, yeah. I'm fine." She went back to rifling through her hockey bag. "Well, I guess I am kind of nervous. What if the boys are too good? Or they get rough? Or what if they never pass to us?"

"It'll be fine," Alyssa said. "It's just for fun. They won't get rough. Why would they?"

Jill wasn't so sure, but before she had time to think about it, there was a knock at the door. A woman peered into the room.

"Everyone decent? Yes? Okay, good." She slipped into the room carrying a big box. "All right, boys," she called back over her shoulder, "everyone is dressed. Come in and we'll go over the rules. Girls, squish over. Believe it or not, this is the bigger dressing room."

Six boys walked into the room and sat down.

"I'm Coach Kelly," the woman said. "That's my son, Griffin."

A boy at the end waved to everyone.

"Let's see if I can remember the rest of you: Jacob, Logan, Dylan, Wade and Luke, right? Plus Griffin, that's six."

The boys nodded.

"Okay, girls, raise your hand if you're here: Alyssa, Camille, Jillian, Lily, Macy and Teagan? Is that right?"

Jill raised her hand. "You can call me Jill."

"Excellent, I will. First things first, welcome to VVA, the smallest rink in Canada!"

The boys cheered sarcastically.

"No, seriously, it's tiny. There's no need to split the rink for three-on-three, so it's perfect for the game. Let's quickly go over the rules. First, there are three skaters and a goalie on the ice for play. And there has to be two girls on the ice all the time. There were enough players for six teams, and each team has a girl goalie."

"Yeah!" Wade said.

Everyone looked at him.

"Oh, I usually play in goal," he explained. "It's time for me to score some goals!"

Coach Kelly smiled. "Awesome, and thanks, Teagan, for playing goal for us."

Everyone cheered for Teagan.

"Next, no slapshots. And no body contact of any

kind from boys or girls. Boys can score two goals in a row, but then a girl has to score a goal. So, boys, if you don't pass to the girls, we may never score more than two. If a boy scores a third goal, it's a penalty. This is all new, so you guys and girls get to be the guinea pigs."

Some of the players snorted like pigs.

"I said *guinea* pigs," Coach Kelly said. "We will keep the shifts as short as possible. You will be tired. It'll be hot. And there's a lot of ice to cover, even if the rink is smaller than normal. Finally, your jerseys."

The coach ripped the tape off the box and started tossing jerseys to the players.

"You're the Rockets," Coach Kelly said. "Every team is named after a Western Hockey League Junior team: Rockets, Giants, Royals, Blazers, Cougars, Bruins and Ice. You'll play one game against each team. Today, we are playing against the Ice. Okay, everyone, let's have fun."

Jill's heart was racing and her hands were sweaty as the team filed into the hallway.

Lily pushed open the gate and they skated out. Jill watched as players from both teams started filtering onto the ice. They zigzagged through their zones in a loose warm-up.

Jill went to the bench. She stood her extra stick in a corner and placed the water bottles along the boards. Alyssa skated up to her and crashed into her shoulder.

"Boo-yah!"

"That's two minutes for that hit, number 15," Jill said with a smile.

"C'mon, get your feet moving, girl."

Jill and Alyssa skated along the centre line, down the right-wing boards and behind the net a couple of times.

Coach Kelly arrived on the bench and dumped a bucket of pucks onto the ice. Rockets players swooped in to retrieve one each.

Jill skated up to the bench again. "Hey, Coach, do you want me to run a warm-up drill?"

"Nah," replied the coach. "The game will start in a minute or two. Just make sure you're warm. We don't want any injuries."

Jill shrugged. She wasn't sure what to do without a structured warm-up to follow. "Okay."

Jacob threw up a shower of ice and snow as he skidded to a stop. He tossed an extra stick onto the bench, grabbed water from a bottle and washed off his mouthguard. He lifted his face mask, bit down on the mouthguard and spit near where Jill was standing.

"Kick the tires and light the fires," he said. "Am I right, Coach?"

"You got it." Coach Kelly reached back to grab her coffee cup. Then she walked off to talk with someone watching from the stands.

Jill was about to ask about strategy when the ref blew his whistle.

Open Ice

The Rockets gathered at the bench. Most of them talked loudly about how many goals they were going to score.

"Anyone know the other team?" Lily asked.

"Yeah, I know a few of them," Logan said. "They're okay, but whatever. Hey, first three on the ice."

Jill watched as Logan, Alyssa and Jacob raced to centre ice. Jill stayed on the bench. Without the support of a coach or a team captain, playing spring hockey didn't feel much like the game she had come to love.

5 Game 1 of 6: GETTING WARMER

Jill sat on the bench, waiting for the game to start. The rest of the team, except for the starting line, piled in next to her.

The referee blew his whistle again and dropped the puck.

Jill looked over her shoulder at Coach Kelly. She was laughing with her friend and not paying much attention to the game.

Jill turned back to watch Jacob win the faceoff and send the puck back to Logan. Then Jacob skated slowly back toward his own net. Jill was confused. She was told three-on-three hockey was an action-packed shootout. All she could see were players looping slowly around the ice as Logan held the puck behind the net.

Finally, Alyssa faked to her right, then cut to her left and into the middle of the ice. Logan passed up the right wing where Alyssa could catch up to the puck. She was able to get around a defender. Suddenly Jill saw the whole ice surface open up in front of Alyssa.

"Go, Alyssa!" Jill shouted.

But Alyssa was alone. Logan was too far behind the play and Jacob's defender was keeping close to him.

Alyssa banked the puck behind her off the boards. Her defender overskated the puck, but then got into a defensive position rather than chase after Alyssa.

That gave Jacob the time he needed to help her. Alyssa saw that he had some open ice, so she dumped the puck back across to him.

Jacob grabbed the puck and charged into the other team's zone. But then he slowed down until he was nearly still.

"Why didn't he shoot?" Jill asked Macy.

"If he misses and they get the puck, he's really far out of position," Macy said.

Jill was still trying to figure out the strategy when Jacob backhanded the puck across the ice. But there was no one on his team there.

Jill panicked. "What's he doing?"

Just as she spoke, Logan swooped into view and scooped up the loose puck. He cut into the slot and faked a shot to get the goalie out of position. Then he lifted the puck over the goalie's leg pad.

Jill nearly jumped off the bench. "Whoa, amazing! How did they do that? How did they know that would work?" She felt like she had when she first started playing. Everyone else seemed to know exactly what they were doing.

When it was time for a line change, Jill took the ice. She wondered how she was going to follow a goal like that. It was her first shift, but Jill had to pull her glove off her hand to wipe away the sweat that had rolled into her eye. Coach Kelly was right. It was hot, and Jill hadn't even played yet.

She lined up along the left wing across from the girl on the other team. Wade was about to take the faceoff and Dylan was playing defence. Jill wasn't sure if she was in the right spot. She looked around for help, but Coach Kelly was still busy talking to her friend in the stands, and Wade was trying to make everyone on the ice laugh.

Jill looked over at the right wing and saw it was completely empty. She kept thinking that, if the other team won the faceoff, they couldn't cover that side. If she left to cover it, though, she would be leaving a player open. Jill looked back at Dylan and shouted to him, "Am I in the right spot?"

"I dunno," he shouted back. "It looks okay to me."

Jill wanted to ask about the open side when the ref dropped the puck. The Ice won it and Jill froze. She couldn't decide where she was needed most. She wanted to chase the puck, but she knew it would take too long to get there. She wanted to stay on the other Ice forward, but there was a lot of empty space between the puck and Teagan in goal. So she decided to drop back a little and help Dylan on defence.

It felt odd to Jill. Not only was she not defending another player, but also there was a lot of room to cover. There was no way she could do it all.

The Ice players were doing what her Rockets had done. They slowly skated around. They passed back and forth, like they were waiting for another player to jump over the boards and into the play.

While Dylan and Jill did their best to look like they had the whole Rockets zone covered, Wade was doing the opposite. He was racing back and forth between players like a dog chasing a ball. The Ice had no trouble passing around him.

Jill wasn't sure Wade was going to last. He was already slowing down, even though the play had just started. He was a distraction, at least, causing so much confusion the Ice didn't get to the Rockets' blue line.

Jill started to push forward and Dylan followed. Now, the three Rockets were closer together. The Ice centre must have been getting frustrated, because he tried to get past Wade along the right wing. But Wade got the toe of his blade on the Ice player's stick, knocking the puck forward just enough that Dylan could pounce.

Jill watched as Dylan jumped into the play and won the puck. He protected it with his back to the boards.

Jill skated toward the middle of the ice where Dylan could get a pass to her. She was alone when Dylan looked up. But instead of passing to Jill, he decided to skate with the puck toward her. Jill moved away and Dylan turned to face the Ice's goal.

"Dilly!" Wade shouted from up the ice. Dylan smacked a hard pass up the middle toward the right wing. Wade just barely got his stick to it. Jill could tell Wade was exhausted. Jill herself was sweating, but hadn't been skating as hard as Wade.

Wade struggled to keep the puck in the Ice's zone. Jill charged up the left wing, but it was too late. The Ice defence was two against one. They chopped at the puck, but Wade managed to get his skate in front of it. It spun quickly into centre ice and Jill was there. Suddenly, she had the puck with just one defender to beat.

She remembered what Macy had said about Jacob. She knew if she tried a shot and missed, she would be giving the puck away. So she drifted to her left, looking for a pass. Dylan provided it. He raced through the centre of the ice and Jill floated the puck ahead of him. He grabbed it and Jill surged ahead. She was alone at the left post.

"Dilly!" she called, trying to imitate Wade's urgency. But Dylan didn't pass to her. Instead, he shot the puck. *What?* Jill thought. *There's a defender right in front of you.*

The goalie kicked out her left pad for an easy save. But the rebound was right there. Wade snapped it home.

"Yeah!" he shouted. "Nice work, Dilly!"

The trio came together to celebrate, but Jill was a little angry. Dylan had been out of position and Wade exhausted. Jill had been wide open.

"If you need it next time, I was wide open," Jill said.

"We didn't need a girl goal yet," Dylan said.

Jill was about to argue, but she decided to keep quiet. Everyone was excited to play. And who would argue against scoring a goal?

But through the rest of the game, the problem kept happening — even as the Rockets kept scoring. Jill kept wondering why the girls were being ignored until the boys needed them.

"What a win, eh?" Wade said as the game ended.

Jill looked up at the scoreboard: Rockets 11, Ice 5.

Yeah, great for you, Jill thought.

6 Game 2 of 6: HEATING UP

Jill and the Rockets were still buzzing about their first win when they arrived at the arena the following week.

Jill grabbed the bucket of pucks and opened them up for the team. The players grabbed at them like they were chocolate-chip cookies from Nana's oven.

"I'm going to score six goals today," Logan said. "So no more passes. Don't even call my name."

Jill laughed. "Well, that's not very nice! I'm going to only pass today. I won't shoot even once."

"Isn't that like always?" Alyssa teased.

"Not always," Jill said. "Maybe if I pass all the time, we can keep the puck out of our net a little and give Teagan a rest."

Jacob skated up to the bench. "I can't shoot," he said. "I only brought one stick and I can't break it. So I'll probably just skate around."

"What are you going to do if your stick breaks?" Logan said.

"Who knows? Maybe I get a day off. Then you guys will have to win by yourselves."

The players laughed and took off from the bench with pucks on their sticks. Jill still didn't understand their warm-ups. Why was everyone so happy to just shoot pucks off the glass or zoom around the ice trying their shootout moves? Jill always loved warm-ups because they helped her get better. Here, there was a lot of kidding around, and the team seemed more into practical jokes than practice.

"Can I see the captains, please?" the ref called from centre ice.

Jill looked around. No one was paying any attention, so she skated over to Coach Kelly on the bench.

"Coach, they need a captain at centre," Jill said.

The coach put her phone into her pocket and looked up at the ice. "Looks like Jacob has it covered."

Jacob was laughing and joking with the other team and the referee. As he skated away from centre, he called all the Rockets to the bench. "Hey, c'mon in for a second."

The players gathered around Jacob, who fastened the strap on his helmet. "There's only one referee today," he said. "The other one's stuck in traffic or has a broken-down car or something. The ref just wants us to know we'll start with one, and hope the other guy gets here soon."

Jill thought that Jacob didn't sound anything like

the boy who wasn't even going to play two weeks ago. But she couldn't help wondering why he was suddenly acting like the team was his to lead. Jill knew he was the strongest player. But he had just said that he wasn't going to shoot because he didn't want his stick to break. It didn't seem like captain behaviour to her.

She put it out of her mind and grabbed her spot on the bench. Taking a few minutes to watch before she got on the ice helped her get a better understanding of how the other team played. And that helped her feel more confident about her own play.

As usual, the other players scrambled to be the starters. This time, Lily and Jacob were first to centre ice and Logan was third.

Alyssa took a seat next to Jill on the bench. "I will get you guys next time, I promise!"

The game began quickly, and the first thing Jill noticed was Lily. She was skating right alongside Jacob and Logan.

"Look at her go," Jill said to Alyssa.

"Go, Lily!" Alyssa shouted. "Whoo!"

Lily was on defence, and got a pass in the middle of the ice. She settled the puck on her stick. To everyone's surprise, she smacked it at the goal.

Wham! It hit the boards behind the goal hard.

"Nice try!" Jill screamed. She was impressed that Lily had not waited for the boys to score. She just went for a girl goal first!

Open Ice

Logan grabbed the rebound on the right side and circled back so he was facing the play. Lily deked and found some open ice. The girl on the Giants didn't seem to know where Lily was.

Logan passed to Lily, who faked a shot and passed across to Jacob. He faked a shot, too, and passed back to Logan.

"Oh, wow," Jill said as she watched the play from the bench. "This is amazing."

Logan didn't fake a pass. Instead, he snapped home the game's first goal.

"That was awesome," Alyssa said as she celebrated with Jill.

The game kept Jill jumping out on the ice as the Rockets built a lead against the Giants. The first period ended with Jill's team leading 5–2, with Lily scoring the girl goal. The Rockets, with Alyssa scoring, stretched that to 7–5 as the game came down to the final few minutes.

Jill still felt energized as the Rockets line came to the bench for a change. She tapped Alyssa on the shoulder and asked her to hold her water bottle. As Alyssa took it, Jill skipped past her to take the next shift.

"Wait, no fair," Alyssa said. "You tricked me!"

"I have to get out here and help the D!" Jill said, laughing.

Jill was still smiling as she turned to see the puck skipping toward her. She put her stick down just in time to receive the pass. She was pinched along the boards, and wanted to get into centre ice to give herself space to pass. One thing she had seen quickly was that passes in three-on-three were often really long.

She moved along the centre line, but there was no one open to receive a pass. The other team was content to stay in their own zone, right in front of their goalie.

Jill skated forward a bit and her teammates looped back toward her. The Giants defence was close to her teammates, so Jill held the puck. She kicked once or twice and glided into the other team's zone.

Her defender still wasn't really moving, standing alone in front of the other team's net. So Jill skated deeper toward the goal.

She curled around, turning her back to the net. But that didn't get the defender to move, either. So Jill cut on a sharp angle and went for a hard skate around the back of the other team's net. This time, the defender went to meet her on the other side. Jill could see she was about to get cut off, so she backhanded the puck behind her. It clicked off the boards and she picked it up again. She turned and skated with it back the other way. On her old team, she might have already tried for a goal by now. But the Rockets expected the girls to wait for chances for girl goals. What should she do?

It was then she spotted Logan coming off the bench on a quick change. He faked going down the wing, but instead cut into the centre of the ice. Jill was all alone and able to feed him an easy pass.

Logan was nearly skating at full speed when he snapped home a shot over the goalie's glove, off the post and into the net.

"Yeah! Wow, that was awesome," she said as Logan came over to give her a high-five.

They skated back to the bench as a line. Jill was smiling so wide that her mouth hurt.

The clock was running down to the final few seconds, and the Rockets were about to win their second game 8–5. There was no time for another faceoff, so the Rockets celebrated at their bench.

"Awesome goal, you guys," Alyssa said.

"Thanks," Logan said. "I thought for sure it was going high. And then — *bam* — it hit the post and went in."

"But you wouldn't have scored at all if it wasn't for that pass, right?" said Jacob.

Jill couldn't believe what she heard. She was pretty sure Jacob was saying she made a nice play. She looked at Logan, but he didn't seem to get it.

"Yeah, I gave Jill a high-five," he said. "The pass was a bit behind me, but it was good."

"Dude, you know this is hockey, right?" Jacob scolded. "Hockey players always thank the set-up man — or woman."

That's exactly what Jill had been going to say.

Jacob was sticking up for her, but did she need someone to do that? She was just about to interrupt when the buzzer sounded. The players spilled from the bench to shake hands with the Giants.

Next time, she thought.

7 Game 3 of 6: ICY HOT

Next up for Jill and the Rockets were the Royals. Jill thought she was early getting out of the girls' dressing room. But she turned a corner to see Jacob taping a stick at the door to the ice. Logan was stretched out in the stands.

Jacob had draped his jacket over his hockey bag and placed a water bottle near him on a bench. He looked completely relaxed.

The Zamboni driver was on all fours just inside the rink, staring at something on the ice. A mound of snow was piled not far from where he was crouched.

"Can this guy go any slower?" Jacob whispered to Jill.

Alyssa appeared behind Jill. "Hey, brother, when's parkour practice? Or are you excited about playing this game?"

"When you win your second game, it tends to put you in a good mood," Jacob answered, smiling. "Scoring eight goals doing it doesn't hurt, either."

"Whoa, I like this new Jake," Logan said. "But you only scored three of those goals, remember?"

"Details, details. It's all about the team."

"Now I'm worried. Lys, call your mom. She needs to take Jake to the hospital. Clearly, he's hit his head or he's been possessed by aliens."

The door banged open behind them and more players filed into the arena.

"What's everyone looking at?" Lily said.

"My brother," Alyssa explained. "He's, like, happy or something."

"Oh, that's weird," Lily said. "I'm scared."

Jacob made a smooshed-up funny-scary face at them. Lily and Alyssa laughed.

"Why is everyone so shocked?" Jill asked. "Jacob was our captain last game. I think he's really enjoying this."

Jill wanted to see what Jacob would do with everyone watching him. She still could not figure out why he sometimes seemed so angry about hockey when he was so good at it. If she was as good as he was, Jill thought, she would never be sad a day in her life.

"Have your fun," Jacob said. "Why is everyone so interested in me, anyway?"

Logan twirled over to his friend, put his hands under his chin and batted his eyelashes like he was staring at a movie star. "Oh, Jake, can I have your autograph?"

Jacob's face turned a little sour. Jill was worried he

might lash out at them. Instead, he just kept taping his stick.

"I guess that's it," Alyssa said. "He does like playing with us. Otherwise, why would he be here so early getting ready?"

"If I wasn't here, you would have lost the first two games," Jacob said.

"Ohhh, is that right, Mr. Hockey?" Logan said.

"Yup, I'm here for you guys. I don't really care about hockey that much. I still might not play next year."

Jill wondered if Jacob really might give up on hockey, right when he could be going to higher levels. But then the Zamboni driver popped up from ice level.

"There's a giant crack in the ice," he said. "Give it at least ten minutes to really freeze. This old barn does not like spring hockey."

Jill thought Jacob looked like a puppy dog that had just lost its favourite toy. But she didn't think about it again until the game was nearly finished.

★★★

"Let's go team, we've got ten minutes to play," Coach Kelly shouted. "Eight to two? Hey, are we really winning by that much?"

Jill shook her head as she took to the ice. The coach

was having fun. The players were having fun. But the team barely talked to each other. The players just rolled off the bench. Positions didn't matter. There wasn't much strategy. And they didn't care about line combinations.

Jill had just stepped onto the ice to replace Macy when the puck came to her. There were no Royals defenders around, so she skated at their goalie. Finally, one of the girls from the Royals came to check her. Jill expected a hard check or an active stick in the passing lane, but the other girl just stopped. Jill curled with the puck on her stick and dumped it back toward Griffin. Together they cleared the Royals' zone. *That was too easy*, Jill thought. *Is it that they don't see me as a scoring threat? Or that they just don't care if we score again.*

Jill had so much room she could skate a big loop around the right wing. She came back to Griffin, who still had the puck. Jill looked at him, and then skated hard away from the play. Griffin flipped a looping pass ahead of Jill, who had all kinds of time and space to choose her next play.

Jill watched as Griffin left and Jacob came onto the ice. The quick change seemed to fool the defence, who didn't pick up Jacob as he skated into the Royals' zone. Jill skated toward the goal line and the defender followed her. Jill raised her stick like she was going to shoot. But she was still bothered by the idea that the Royals didn't think she could score. Maybe they were right.

So she passed the puck behind her into the slot.

The pass was perfect. With a smile on his face, Jacob cut into the slot and smacked home a one-timer that zipped toward the goalie's five-hole. *But it's time for a girl goal*, Jill thought. *Doesn't Jacob care that he will get a penalty if he scores?*

The puck hit the goalie's pads and just sat there, spinning on the goal line. Jill was the first to spot it. She felt herself leave her skates and dive forward, headfirst, at the net. She got to the puck as the goalie was reaching back. Jill nudged it across the red line for a goal.

"What?" she yelled as she stood. "I can't believe it!"

"Atta girl, Jill!" crowed Alyssa. "Your first Rockets goal!"

"Told ya," Jacob said. "This team needs me."

8 CRACKS IN THE ICE

Their next game was against the Cougars. The teams were evenly matched and neither had scored yet.

Jill's legs burned as she chased the puck carrier deep into her own zone. Jacob was alone defending a two-on-one. Jill was sure she could catch up to help him and Teagan in goal.

"Here, here!" the Cougars forward yelled.

The puck carrier started to slow. Jacob eased off to block the pass and Teagan came out to challenge the shooter.

That was the break Jill needed. There was no way she wanted the Rockets to lose after three straight wins. The Cougars shooter pulled her stick back. Jill lunged forward, but she was still too far away. The Cougar snapped a zippy shot from the hash marks of the left faceoff circle. Jill had the perfect view of the puck slicing through the air and ringing hard off the post behind Teagan.

Clang!

The puck ricocheted off the post and crashed into the glass behind the Rockets' net. It was going so quickly, the flying rebound forced the referee to duck. Jill watched the puck deflect off the glass along the wing and back out toward the Rockets' blue line.

Jill slammed on the brakes, showering the ice with snow. She pushed left skate over right, trying to turn as fast as she could. It seemed to be working. She felt herself gaining speed and catching up to the puck as it wobbled through the neutral zone.

The Cougars defender took a half-step, but Jill was coming through quickly.

"Not today," Jill said. She was excited. She didn't care if it was time for a boy goal or a girl goal. This play was hers.

She picked up the puck. Suddenly the Rockets had a two-on-one going the other way. Wade was on her right as Jill skated toward the Cougars' blue line. She could sense her teammates on the bench standing to watch.

She could hear high-pitched shouting and screaming from both benches. She heard the air rushing past her helmet and buzzing in her ears. Wade's voice finally cut through the noise.

"Jilly, Jilly," he screamed.

The play was the exact opposite of what had just happened at the other end of the rink. The Cougars knew a boy could score, so the defender backed off to block Jill's pass. The goalie came out to challenge Wade.

Jill didn't want to miss and give the puck away. She didn't have nearly enough energy to make it back to play defence.

The Rockets really needed to score the first goal.

Jill took a chance and snapped a pass over to Wade. But with a defender leaning that direction, he didn't have much to shoot at.

But the play worked. It got the attention off of Jill. "Wade!" she called.

The goalie pushed off toward her left post, expecting Wade to shoot. Jill was looking at a wide open net. All that Wade needed to do was find a passing lane back and Jill would have an easy goal.

It was like Wade read Jill's mind. In one smooth motion, he received the pass and floated it back to Jill over the defender's stick.

Jill practically slid on her knees to get to the right place. She crouched down low, held the blade of her stick firm and let the puck hit her stick and bank into the net.

"Whoo!" she yelled.

The referee blew her whistle and pointed to the net: "Goal!"

"Wow, what an amazing pass, Wade!" Jill said. They coasted into the glass, celebrating as they went with hugs and taps to the helmet.

"Your pass was better," Wade said. "Good thing you gave it to me early. That gave me time to get it back to you."

They could have had two boy goals before they needed a girl goal. Jill almost couldn't believe that Wade had given her the chance to score. And she was exhausted as she skated to the bench for a line change. Jacob was on her right and Alyssa on her left as they sat down.

"Great D," she finally said to Jacob.

"Nice goal," he said.

Like an echo, the referee shouted, "Goal!" from the ice. The Cougars were celebrating.

Jill couldn't figure out what had happened.

"The Cougars scored off the faceoff," Alyssa said. "They just skated right to our net and scored."

"What?" Jill was amazed. "It's been, like, two seconds."

"Yeah, it was pretty fast."

The teams lined up, and almost as easily the Cougars won the faceoff again. Jill watched as the Cougars held the puck for what felt like two minutes, passing around the Rockets' zone like there was no defence.

Zip-zap-zoom — "Goal!"

When Jill had come to the bench, she was ready to celebrate and replay her goal with her teammates. Now, only a few minutes later, they were losing 2–1.

Jill took her place at right wing for her next shift. Jacob took the faceoff. Jacob won it back along Wade's wing, and Jill curled back to get into position for a pass.

The Cougars were full of energy, and two forwards

moved into position to trap Wade. His only option was to bank it off the boards on the left wing and hope someone had enough time to get there. Jill took off from the right wing, thinking Jacob would chip it up to her.

Jacob got to the puck and banged at it, but he hit it too hard. Jill tried to trap it along the boards with her shin pads or skates. But it skipped through her legs and into the Cougars' zone.

The Cougars defender easily picked it up. With Jill out of position, the defender skated around his net. He took two strides forward and smashed a hard, low pass up the ice. It went right where Jill should have been.

The Cougars forward picked up the puck on the wing. She was wide open, and the Cougars needed a girl to score. Jacob tried to skate back and reach around her with his stick. But the fast-skating forward blocked him with her leg. She chipped the puck up over Teagan's pads.

"Goal!" the ref said, pointing to the goal.

Jill skated back to the faceoff circle as the Cougars celebrated again.

"Don't get caught out of position this time," Jacob told her.

"Don't smash the puck over my stick!"

"All right, let's not worry about it," Wade said as they skated to the bench.

"I'm not worried," Jill said.

But she knew that was a lie. She was worried about the way Jacob snapped at her. She was worried their fourth game was not going to end well.

"Maybe you should be," Jacob said, echoing her thoughts.

Jill bit down on her mouthguard, trying to think of something positive to say. It didn't work. She kept stewing as the game went on and the Cougars kept scoring. The score went from 4–1 to 5–2, and all the way to a final score of 8–4.

Jill and Jacob kept trading accusations and insults the entire game. Finally, Jill said what was really bugging her. She cornered Jacob just as they were about to leave the ice after the game.

"You don't trust the girls, do you?"

"What? Of course I do. It's just that you don't want to take instructions."

"Oh, no way, I keep asking the coach for help."

"Don't bother. The coach is letting us figure this out. And who cares, anyway? It's three-on-three. It's not even real hockey."

Jill shook her head and stalked off the ice. *Not real hockey?* she kept thinking. *This is the best hockey I've ever played.*

But she also felt guilty. Was Jacob trying to help her? She thought back to the games they had played. If he was trying to help her, he had a funny way of showing it.

9 Game 5 of 6:
SHE SHOOTS, SHE SCORES

Jill was not going to let the team's first loss ruin her good mood.

Truth be told, she enjoyed playing a tougher team. She told her teammates they should be proud of how well they played when they arrived at the rink for the next game.

"We lost, but the score was only 8–4," she said. "I think if we had more time, we could have tied it. Our girls were way better than their girls." She didn't mention her surprise first goal of the game, scoring a "boy goal." She thought about what skilled players Alyssa and Lily were. Way more skilled than Jill. And Teagan was a big part of every win they had.

In our four games so far, Jill thought, *it's the girls who made a difference.*

The other teams had to wait for a long time between the second goal by a boy and the time a girl scored. But the Rockets had been able to get goals from their girls much sooner. What would happen if Alyssa and Lily tried to score before the boys had scored twice? That would allow the whole team to play as hard as they could for the entire time.

"Maybe we shouldn't worry about the girls scoring after the boys," she said to the team. "Maybe we should just all play as hard as we can until somebody scores."

Logan and Jacob started to laugh. And it wasn't fake laughing. Jill could tell they really thought what she said was funny.

"I know you scored first last game, Jill," said Logan. "But that was a fluke. We can't base team strategy on that."

What team strategy? Jill thought. But she didn't say anything. She just squeezed her stick as tightly as she could.

She was still trying to forget about the boys' reaction when the first period started. Jill was sure the best way to deal with her rude teammates was to prove to them she was right.

She looked across the ice at the other team: the Bruins. She didn't recognize any of the players. It made her feel better that she didn't know any of them. *Good*, she thought, *I won't feel guilty when we cream them.*

Jill stood near the faceoff dot through most of the warm-up. She was going to win the team's race to centre at the start of the game. She barely said anything when Jacob — as usual — arrived right after the whistle.

"Hey, that's not fair," he said. "You were standing here the whole time."

"Sometimes, Jacob," Jill said, "life is not fair." She turned to take her place on the right wing.

Jacob skated to centre for the faceoff. He won it cleanly back to Logan. Jill skated slowly back behind him, trying to lose her defender.

It was a trick the team had used before, and Logan was ready.

Jacob skated hard toward the other team's blue line, smacking his stick on the ice like he wanted the pass. It didn't matter how close the other team was, Logan faked like he was going to pass it to Jacob. But Jacob slammed on his brakes and charged hard back toward the centre of the rink.

That's when Logan made a hard pass up the middle.

Jill, meanwhile, kept skating along the right wing. Jacob tipped the puck instead of taking the pass. The puck zipped right in front of Jill. She didn't look up, she just skated as hard as she could. She caught up to the puck and held it along the right faceoff circle in the Bruins' zone.

In other games, unless it was a girl goal, the girl with the puck in the zone would pass across to a boy, either the centre skating hard to the goal or the defender.

The Bruins must have seen the play before, because one of them was all over Jacob as he crashed the net. Remembering the surprise first goal of the game she scored against the Cougars, Jill didn't want to pass to Jacob.

Jacob curled out of the way, thinking he needed to stay close to the net for a rebound if Logan missed.

Logan came barrelling through next. This time, two defenders went to him.

Good, Jill thought. *I don't want to pass to him, either.*

But Jill didn't want anyone to know she wanted to keep the puck. She faked passes as best she could both times. And both times, even her teammates were fooled.

Then Jill made her move. She took two big strides toward the net and ripped a wrist shot. The puck raced to the far side of the net and went in just below the goalie's glove.

"Yeah!" Jill roared.

She stood and raised her arms in the air. Jacob and Logan skated toward her. Their mouths were so wide open that Jill thought they could fit a puck inside each one.

"Whoa," Logan said. "Where did that come from?"

Jill didn't say what she wanted to say. She didn't tell them she was mad at them — so mad that she had just shot the puck as hard as she could. Instead, she gave them each fist bumps. "Now, you guys can score a couple."

She really hoped they understood what she was trying to show them. The kind of advantage playing the girls could give their team. She skated back to the bench where Alyssa was there to grab her.

"Amazing!" said Alyssa.

"Thanks," Jill said.

"Where did you learn to shoot so hard?"

"Logan and Jacob made me mad."

"Cool," Alyssa said with a smile. "I'll have to make sure they get you mad before every game."

Jill cracked a smile. Her good mood was back. And it got even better with twin goals by Jacob and Alyssa. A surprise goal by Macy gave the Rockets a 4–0 lead in the first ten minutes of the game. The other team kept trying to score, but the Rockets were loose and relaxed. Jill knew it had all started with a girl scoring first. And how that made the girls on the team see that they shouldn't hold back. She hoped Jacob and Logan noticed it.

The Rockets went on to win 10–5. The girls on the team racked up five of those goals, and Jill had lost track of whether they were girl goals or not. It was their best game yet.

"Good game," she said to Jacob and Logan as they waited in the lobby for their ride.

"Yeah, thanks," Jacob said. "Hey, Logan, you and I each got two goals and two assists."

"And I got a goal and an assist," Jill said, interrupting them. "I got the first goal, remember? We were able to lead early."

Logan looked at Jacob. Jacob looked back at Logan. Neither looked at Jill. "Oh, now I get it," Jacob said.

"Okay, maybe you're right, Jill. But you're never going to score another one like that. That will probably be your best ever."

Jill's bad mood was back. "Not if I get motivated again," she said, frowning. "And I think I'll have lots of motivation playing with you two."

10 Game 6 of 6: NO TROPHIES

Jill had to double-check the schedule. She couldn't believe the season was already coming to an end.

"Why do we only play six games? That doesn't seem like enough," Jill told Alyssa as they warmed up together. "We should play three-on-three all winter long. I wasn't sure I'd like it, but it is really fun. And I think my play is better, too."

Alyssa nodded her head as they swooped behind the net for another lap around the ice. "Yeah," Alyssa said. "There isn't the same kind of pressure to win. I don't think Coach Kelly has said two words to us all season. She just drinks coffee and talks to the parents. She should just let us handle everything. What could go wrong?"

"It's true," Jill said. "Even the refs are in good moods."

Coach Kelly called the Rockets to the bench. "Okay, team, this has been a blast. Enjoy your last game, and then we'll talk about arrangements for the Kelowna tournament. I need everyone's permission forms if you're not going with a parent."

Jill was not interested in racing to centre ice for the starting faceoff. She quietly shuffled onto the bench to watch the first few minutes. With the short shifts, there was always a lot of playing time. She didn't need to worry about being first on the ice.

She was surprised, though, to see Jacob stepping off the ice and sitting near her.

"Why are you here?" Jill asked.

"Uh, because I'm playing," he said.

"No, I mean on the bench. You usually like to start."

"Not always."

Jill wasn't sure she believed him. She thought he looked nervous. Once the game started, she thought she had her answer. The boys on the Blazers could skate and shoot just like Jacob and Logan. She saw that some of the players were members of the team that beat Jacob's team in the last game of the regular hockey season. They were fast and could change directions as easily as skating straight.

Jill watched Alyssa, one of the best girls she had ever seen play hockey, hold the puck along the boards. Alyssa was looking for a pass when one of the Blazers boys came swooping into the play. He stole the puck and skated away in one motion.

"Hey, let the girls play!" Jacob shouted from the bench.

"Why did you say that?" Jill asked.

"If there's two girls fighting for the puck, I stay away.

It's just not cool, what that guy did."

Jill wasn't sure how she felt about that. Was it the nicest thing she had ever heard him say? Or was he saying girls couldn't compete with boys?

Jacob was still standing as the Blazers skated at Teagan in goal. It was a two-on-one, and the two boys passed back and forth before one of them raised his stick.

"Don't you dare," Jacob shouted, standing on the bench.

Jill was confused again. The Blazer lowered his stick a bit, but still snapped the puck hard at Teagan. It whizzed past her helmet and she had to duck to avoid getting hit in the mask.

"Oh!" Jacob shouted. "That was a slapshot! Ref!"

Jill could suddenly feel tension on the bench. Now the referee and Coach Kelly were paying attention to Jacob's shouting.

"What's going on?" the coach asked.

"That guy is a jerk," Jacob said. "He nearly hit Teagan with a slapshot!"

"I'm sure it was an accident, Jacob. Don't lose your cool. Let the ref handle it."

"No slapshots, ref," Jacob shouted again.

It seemed to Jill like it was the wrong way for Jacob to keep his cool. The referee didn't blow his whistle. The Blazers kept the puck in the zone. They looped around the Rockets' net before one of the boys scored on a wrist shot.

"I want on," Jacob said. He moved past two other players to stand at the gate. But before he could get onto the ice, the Blazers skated past their bench.

"Whooo! Did you see that shot, Tate?" one of them taunted Jacob. "Your goalie didn't."

Jill watched as they went to their bench for high-fives. When Jacob went straight to centre ice, Jill followed him. She was more nervous than she had been since the start of the spring season.

Jacob won the faceoff easily. Jill skated to her right and picked up the puck. She sent a quick pass back to Dylan on defence.

She thought they were going to try their favourite play, so she looped back behind. Jacob did his part by skating from the other wing, banging his stick on the ice. But instead of clearing from the centre of the ice, he stayed there yelling at Dylan for the puck.

Jill could only watch as Dylan forced the pass up the centre.

The Blazers defenders deflected it away easily.

Jacob banged his stick on the ice in anger. He chased the puck to the wing, but the Blazers just passed it around him.

Jill and Dylan were back as the Blazers broke into the Rockets' zone three-on-two. Jill followed the girl on the left wing, but the Blazers player just stood there.

Dylan moved to his right to take away the pass and let Teagan see the shooter. But Teagan didn't stand much of a chance against the Blazers forward. He picked the corner over her shoulder and suddenly the Rockets were losing 2–0.

"*Whoooo*, another one!" the goal scorer shouted.

Jacob finally came flying back on defence, but he was too late. He went straight to the net, fished out the puck and shot it down the ice.

"You guys wanna play like that?" he asked the Blazers.

"What, you mean like awesome?" The forward dismissed Jacob by turning his back.

"You guys are going to that Kelowna tournament?" the Blazers forward asked. "You're going to get smashed. You guys are going to embarrass yourselves."

Jill couldn't believe how rude they were being. Why? There were no trophies to compete for. This was supposed to be for fun. She was suddenly worried Jacob was going to do something stupid to get back at the Blazers forward. She had to step in.

"Don't worry about us," Jill interrupted. "The only embarrassing thing around here is the way you're acting."

Dylan turned to look at Jill. She could tell he was surprised she was getting mixed up in things. Too bad it didn't calm things down at all.

Now, Jacob and Dylan were shoulder to shoulder. They were shouting and pointing fingers back and forth with the boys from the Blazers.

Jill wanted to be anywhere but on the ice.

11 Going Out with A BANG

Jill looked up at the scoreboard: Blazers 5, Rockets 4.

Twice the Blazers had scored two goals quickly in a row. And twice the Rockets were able to catch up because the Blazers were waiting for their girls to score. Maybe the girls on the Blazers were not as good as the girls on the Rockets. Or they were not trying as hard. Or maybe they were told to try only when they needed to score.

There were eight minutes left to play, and the clock wouldn't stop for a whistle. The running clock was part of what made three-on-three hockey so much fun. It made it feel like they were playing a video game. The end of a game always felt like a race against time.

But this time, Jill just wanted the game to end as quickly as possible.

The boys on the two teams were still bickering. Their voices carried everywhere on the ice. Jill kept looking at the referee and Coach Kelly, and neither of them seemed to care. Why didn't they stop this?

Wasn't it against the rules to shout at the other team?

It made Jill think the boys on her team were too distracted to worry about playing the game. She had given up thinking this game would be fun.

Jill skated into the Blazers' end for a faceoff. She took her spot along the right wing. Logan was on defence and Jacob was taking the faceoff. He won it, but the puck went into a corner with no one there. Jill was closest, so she pumped her legs as fast as she could. She was certain she could get the puck first and fire it out front of the Blazers' goal. From there, Jacob might tip it into the net.

She could see from the corner of her eye the red jersey of a Blazers defender on her left. Jill collected the puck along the boards and tried to skate to her right, away from the defence.

But Jill didn't get very far. She crashed into something and fell to the ice. She was lying on the ice, trying to figure out what had happened. She knew she had not hit the boards. She thought at first the referee might have been too close. She tried to stand on her skates but there was something blocking her way.

She looked up. All she could see was a bunch of jerseys above her. Jill was suddenly scared. There was shouting and shoving. Boys were falling over her along the boards. Jill couldn't move very well. She kept slipping.

"You hit her!"

"I did not. She crashed into me."

"Why don't you just let the girls play, you jerk?"

"There's no rule about that, idiot."

Jill realized what had happened. She had crashed into a boy on the Blazers when both of them had come to get the puck.

Jill finally got to her skates.

"Hey, quit it!" she shouted.

It didn't make any difference.

The referee skated over to the corner and blew on her whistle. That didn't stop the boys, either.

Then Jill saw something she had been worried about all game. Jacob took his hand off his stick and punched one of the Blazers in the chest. His glove stayed on, but it was a punch.

The Blazers player did the same back. Jacob lunged at him. They were holding on to each other now. Logan grabbed the Blazers player, and it was two against one. Then another boy from the Blazers got involved. Soon, all four boys were wrestling and shoving. They all collapsed to the ice in a heap.

It got worse. Jacob was on top of a Blazers player, shoving him into the ice. The other boy was doing the same to Logan.

Jill just stood there, shocked.

One of the girls on the Blazers skated over to her. "Our guys do stuff like this all the time," she said.

"They get into fights every game?" Jill asked.

"Well, no. It's never been this bad. But we seem to make everyone angry. I can't believe you haven't heard about our team. I thought everyone had."

"I barely notice who we are playing. I just keep thinking about how much fun three-on-three is."

The referees finally got themselves between the boys. They escorted the players straight to the door that opened to the dressing rooms. Jacob, Logan and two of the Blazers boys were ejected from the game.

"I hate three-on-three," the girl from the Blazers said. "The boys never pass to us. I mean never. At least the boys on your team seem to be trying to protect you, or something."

As she skated back to her bench, Jill realized that she had never thought the boys on her team were trying to be good teammates. But did they think the girls needed protecting?

Jill leaned on the bench and grabbed a water bottle. She looked up at the clock — which had been running the whole time. She watched it tick down to one minute left. The referee skated up to their bench.

"Not much time left," she said to Coach Kelly.

"Yeah, let's just call it a day."

Jill could not believe it. Her final game of the season was ending early. The really short season was ending early. All because some boys could not control their tempers.

Worse than that, the Rockets lost 5–4.

Would that be the final three-on-three game Jill would ever play? She was worried it might be.

12 Caught on VIDEO

Jill heard banging on the front door, then the ringing of the doorbell. Then more banging, followed by more ringing. Jill's dad was at work, and her mom was shouting to her from upstairs to answer the door.

"What if it's a bad guy who is trying to break into our house?" Jill called up.

"You know it's just one of your silly friends."

Jill had to admit, that's exactly what it was. Not only that, Jill knew it was Alyssa. She opened the door to hear, "We're on YouTube. We're on the news."

Alyssa pushed past Jill and into the living room. She paced back and forth around the coffee table. All the while, she muttered to herself something about "embarrassed," "brother" and "hockey."

"What's going on?" Jill asked. "What's wrong?"

Once she caught a look of Alyssa's face, she realized something was really wrong. It was like the time Alyssa's dad's business was sold, or the time her mom crashed her bike.

Alyssa was not saying anything, though. She just kept pacing the living room.

"Will you please tell me what is happening?" Jill said. "You're scaring me."

"Look at this." Alyssa pulled her phone from her pocket. She unlocked it and handed it to Jill.

Jill pressed play on the video. It was grainy, but she could see it was a hockey game. Then she felt the blood draining from her face.

It was the Rockets game against the Blazers. The four boys pushing and shoving above a girl on the ice. That was her. Jill. She was trying to stand up, but kept slipping.

"Why am I such a weirdo?" asked Jill. "Why don't I just stand up?"

Then she remembered what had happened. Every time she tried to get to her feet, she kept tripping on the puck or another player's stick.

She watched Jacob pull his arm back and push it into the other player's chest. The other boy punched back, and then Logan jumped between them. They all fell over and wrestled around on the ice.

The video stopped when the referees finally separated them. The title of the video appeared: "Brawl! Boys push girl in 3-on-3 coed hockey."

Information at the bottom of the video said it had been posted twelve hours before. It had been viewed 17,103 times. It had 392 comments. The first one said,

"How disgusting! Those boys should not be allowed to play hockey ever again."

Jill looked up at Alyssa, who was clutching her hands in front of her face. Jill could see tears beginning to form in her friend's eyes.

"We've gone viral," Alyssa managed to say before she began to sob.

"Has Jacob seen this?"

"Yeah. Logan is at our house with his parents. They saw it first and came over. I'm supposed to ask you and your parents to come over. It was the three of you in the video. My dad said it's important you have a say in what happens next."

Jill and Alyssa walked up the stairs to get Jill's mom. Jill was not sure why, but she was nervous. To Jill's eyes it had not been a real fight, and she hadn't taken part. But she felt sure her mom would never allow her to play hockey again.

Each stair the girls took seemed to creak louder than the one before it. Jill looked at the pictures on the wall, pictures of herself from first to eighth grade. There were pictures of her playing soccer and playing hockey. There were family portraits and pictures of her grandparents.

It made Jill think that her parents must still see her as a little kid. But she wasn't a kid anymore. She was fourteen years old, and she could handle herself at hockey. She had never been hurt or in any danger, even playing with boys.

Whether it was right or not, the boys on her team were trying to protect her. The video was proof.

It all sounded good in Jill's head. But she knew it wasn't going to convince her mom. She knew her parents wouldn't care. Her mom would just say no, and that would be it. Jill hadn't done anything wrong. Why should she be punished?

Jill and Alyssa reached the top of the stairs. *Okay,* Jill thought, *I'm ready.* They took two steps toward the master bedroom and pushed open the door.

Jill's mom was reattaching a curtain rod to the wall. She had a hammer in her hand. Jill froze.

"I didn't think she would have a weapon," she mumbled to Alyssa. "Maybe I should wait."

"Huh? No! Do this now."

Jill swallowed hard and began to tell her the story.

It seemed to take longer than the actual event. Jill kept explaining things. Like how the whistle had gone. And how the game was really close. And how it was the last game of the season.

"And now Alyssa's mom and dad, and Logan's mom and dad, are all at Alyssa's house," Jill said. "And they want you and Dad to go over, too. But we shouldn't call Dad away from work. And I don't know what to do. And Alyssa said something about us being on the news."

Alyssa finally produced the phone from her pocket. They handed it to Jill's mom, who took the phone and pressed play.

Jill could not watch her mom watching the video. She closed her eyes and waited for the explosion of anger. What Jill heard, though, was an explosion of laughter. Then it got even louder.

"Who is the clumsy kid who can't stand up?" laughed her mom.

"Mom! That's me!"

"Oh, you hockey players," her mom said. "I don't understand the game at all. You go tell your parents, Alyssa, that we aren't too worried. We're happy with whatever they want to do. Do we have to pay a fine or something?"

"No, no I don't think so," Alyssa said. "But the news showed it. And they were all like, 'Can you believe what happened during this spring league hockey game?'"

Jill was relieved. There would be no punishment. But she was annoyed, too, that her mom was not showing more concern. Or helping her fix the problem.

"Just because it's on the news doesn't mean it means anything," her mom said.

"Well, the league called us," Alyssa said. "They don't want us going to Kelowna for the tournament."

"You didn't tell me that," Jill said.

"Sorry, I didn't want to make it worse."

Jill wasn't worried anymore. She wasn't nervous. She was angry. And she wanted to go to Alyssa's house and tell Jacob just what she thought of his stupid fight.

13 Letter GRADE

Jill sat on a couch in Alyssa's living room. Why couldn't she just make it all go away?

Everyone was quiet as Alyssa's dad attended the conference call with Coach Kelly and the league commissioner. All Jill could hear was him murmuring "uh-huh" or "yes, of course," or "no, by no means" over and over again. He was a lawyer, and so the team felt like he could best speak to the league about consequences of the fight.

At least the team is in good hands, Jill thought.

Finally, he ended the call and turned to the group. "Good news and bad news," he said. "The league won't punish the players involved. They'll be able to register next year. They might be suspended for a game."

"Is that the good news or the bad news?" Logan asked.

"That's good news," Logan's mom said.

"Yeah, it's good news," Alyssa's dad said. "But they don't want either team going to Kelowna. They think cancelling your registration in the tournament would be a more fitting punishment."

Jill's heart sank. She had been looking forward to their weekend road trip.

"Oh, come on," Alyssa said. "That's punishing the whole team, not just the boys involved."

Her dad nodded his head in agreement. He seemed to understand. But he had that look dads get when there is nothing they can do.

"What about the video?" Alyssa's mom said. "Should we send a statement to the press saying we apologize for the outburst and it won't happen again? Or that the boys involved are being punished?"

Logan's mom shook her head. "I talked to my sister about that," she said. "She's a journalist — in Kelowna, actually. She said it wouldn't help. In fact, she thought it would just give the story a second life. She said a few people in Kelowna were talking about the video, but no one there knows we were supposed to go to the tournament."

Alyssa opened her tablet computer and checked the video's stats. "It's up to 25,994 views," she said. "It's kind of slowing down. Now everyone is just commenting on how Jill keeps stepping on hockey sticks and the puck, and keeps slipping. They're calling it the Bambi Brawl."

There was some muffled snickering from the adults. Jill grabbed a pillow and tried to hide behind it.

"You know, like Bambi on ice in the movie," Alyssa said.

"We know what it means!" Jill said.

"Okay, so no press releases," Logan said. "And we don't have to pay any fines or anything. But what do we do about Kelowna?"

"That's the real question," Alyssa's dad said. "Coach Kelly and the league commissioner are going to talk to the tournament organizers tomorrow and let us know. They said they'll give us time to offer up a plan, too."

The group seemed to be at a loss. Jill couldn't help wondering why Jacob was so quiet. Shouldn't he be apologizing? He was just sitting there, staring into a corner.

Then Jill knew exactly what they should be doing, as a team. They needed to apologize, to accept blame and promise to be better. She also thought there were too many adults involved. All season, Coach Kelly, the parents — everyone — had just let the kids play. Maybe the kids should be the ones who figured this out for themselves.

"I think I have an idea," Jill said. "We need to call a players-only meeting. We will tell you tomorrow what we decide. As a team." She stood and grabbed the team list from the coffee table.

"Cool," Logan said. "It'll be like we're in the NHL. The Canucks are always calling players-only meetings."

"That's not a good thing," Alyssa said. "It means the Canucks are always in trouble."

"I think that is a really great idea, Jill," Alyssa's dad said. "Let us know before noon tomorrow. That's when they want to make a decision. You have less than a day, and tomorrow is school."

The parents stood, said their goodbyes and went their separate ways. Jill looked at the clock. It was four o'clock on Sunday. It meant the team had just a few hours to get organized. Jill was thankful there were only twelve players on the team, and four of them were in the room.

"How are we going to get everyone together in such a short time?" Logan asked, echoing Jill's thoughts.

"We don't have to meet in person," Jill decided. "Alyssa, do you have everyone's contact information on your tablet?"

"Yeah, I think so."

"What's this plan?" Logan asked.

"We need to apologize," said Jill. "We need to promise never to do it again, and offer up some kind of punishment. I think we all need to write letters to the league, asking them to forgive us."

"We need to tell them why sportsmanship is important, too," Alyssa said.

"That's awesome," agreed Logan. "Adults love that stuff."

"We need to volunteer," a voice said. It was Jacob.

Jill's head snapped around. She had not expected Jacob to say anything at all. She had not even expected him to agree to write a letter. Most of all, she never thought he would say something so smart.

"Dude, what are you saying?" Logan said. "That I have to go into an old folks' home and sing to them, like last year in school?"

"Nah," Jacob said. "We should pick up garbage at the park next to the rink. And we should invite the Blazers to join us."

Jill was stunned, and so was everyone else.

"That's awesome," Alyssa said. "My twin brother is sneaky smart."

Jill had to admit that it sounded like just the kind of thing that would work. "I think he's right," she said. "Alyssa and I will use the tablet to contact the girls. We'll ask them to email us letters about why sportsmanship is so important. Logan, you and Jacob should contact the boys from your house. Tell them we need letters emailed to me before tomorrow at noon. I don't want anyone to say they'll send it and not do it. You need to motivate those boys, and we'll do the same with the girls."

Jill was feeling better about the plan. There was no way she would let the Bambi Brawl be the last thing she — or anyone else — remembered from this season.

14 Special DELIVERY

Jill and Alyssa watched the printer in the school office spit out the final letter. Jill collected the sheet and added it to their pile. Jill slipped them all into a plain brown envelope and sealed it.

On the front of the envelope, Alyssa wrote:

To: West Park Minor Hockey.

From: the West Park Rockets.

Jill resisted the urge to add something like *We're so sorry.* Or *Please let us play in Kelowna.* She wanted it to look as professional as possible.

Jill glanced at the clock. It was nearly noon. Coach Kelly had promised to collect the letters from them and deliver them herself. She was taking them to the meeting with the league commissioner and the president of the West Park Minor Hockey Association.

Jill and Alyssa hurried from the library thanking the staff — at first too loudly, and then quietly. Then they bolted for the school's front door.

They waded through a sea of kids on lunch break.

Alyssa was out front, clearing their path. Jill clutched the envelope filled with letters to her chest. She kept looking nervously over her shoulder for teachers. If they were stopped now for running in the hallways, the whole plan might fail.

They finally pushed out the front door and were blinded by sunshine. It was one of those rare spring days in Vancouver when the skies were clear of rain and cloud. The smell of cherry blossoms filled the air and the trees swayed in a gentle breeze. Most kids were kicking a soccer ball, shooting basketballs or just hanging out together. Everyone was in a good mood.

Jill was nervous. It didn't feel like any hockey season she had played. But she was certain she wanted to play more.

Alyssa spotted Coach Kelly walking up the school's front entrance. Jill held out the envelope to her.

"I can't believe you got this done," the coach said. "I didn't think you would get everyone to write a letter on such short notice."

"Well, some of the letters are kind of short," Jill admitted. "But I think they all sound good. I'm very convincing when I need to be."

"Do you actually have everyone?"

"Yup, every last player," Alyssa said. "Jake and Logan were a big help. The boys called the boys, and we talked to the girls. You can get a lot done with video chat."

Coach Kelly tucked the envelope into her briefcase. "Jacob helped?" she asked.

"Yeah, Logan said he didn't just sit there and pout. Apparently, Jake was pretty convincing. I think he was actually having fun this season."

"Let's hope so," Coach Kelly laughed. "If he didn't, then I'm not doing a very good job, and I'm not sure why he's on the team. Okay, I better get going. Enjoy the sunshine and wish me luck."

"You won't need luck," Jill said. "You're going to rock it!"

Jill watched as Coach Kelly got into her minivan. She spotted the envelope peeking from the side pocket of her coach's bag.

What if it falls out? she worried. *Then they'll never let us go to Kelowna.*

But it didn't fall, and Coach Kelly drove away safely. Jill let out a huge sigh of relief.

"Jill, do you think Jake is having fun?" Alyssa asked.

Jill looked at her friend after waving at the coach one last time. "Well, he's an incredible player. I don't get why he's so grumpy sometimes. I wish I had half his talent. I hope he's having fun. Like Coach said, what's the point otherwise? He's not getting paid for this, right?"

"No, of course not. But sometimes I think he's thinking about playing pro. You know, pretending that's what he's doing, even in our three-on-three games."

Jill stared at the ground. It made sense. But she was still confused about Jacob getting angry when the other team crashed into her, or took hard shots on Teagan.

"Then why does he keep trying to protect us? Doesn't he trust us?"

"I dunno," Alyssa said. "Jake and I were on the same team until we were seven. He should know girls can play. But maybe you're right. My dad used to joke about it. He'd tell Jake before every game, 'Don't forget to protect your sister,'" Alyssa added, doing her best "dad" voice.

Jill burst out laughing. "Is your dad Kermit the Frog pretending to be Batman?"

It was Alyssa's turn to laugh her head off. But once the laughter died down, Jill realized she still didn't understand Alyssa's brother.

"Well, we have to tell him to stop worrying about us, then," Jill said. "I could totally be the enforcer for you."

"Yeah, you better. I think it also has to do with Jake always being the best player, always being captain. He really feels that responsibility. He takes it all so seriously. And next year he'll be that much closer to playing Junior. If he doesn't get drafted, my parents are talking about him going to some hockey academy thingy. You go to school in the morning and play hockey in the afternoon."

"Wow, that sounds expensive."

"Yeah, I don't know," Alyssa said. "Dad said I could join, too. But I don't want to switch schools."

As Jill imagined the hockey academy, she felt butterflies gnawing at the inside of her stomach. She could only dream of going to school for hockey. She wondered if Jacob and Alyssa realized how lucky they were to even have that option. "But I thought Jacob was going to quit hockey."

"Nah, no way. My dad says that Jake is just doubting himself. He really wants Jake to try for Junior."

Of course, Jill thought. She remembered Alyssa saying something about the WHL draft. How Jacob and Logan were planning to watch it on their computer.

"When is it? The draft, I mean."

"Soon, I think."

If that's the case, Jill thought, *maybe Jacob can relax after the draft. Or maybe if he isn't drafted, he will be even more angry.* It was too much for Jill to think about.

The sun peeked from behind a wispy cloud and beat down on them. Jill closed her eyes and let it warm her face. Maybe Coach Kelly wouldn't be able to convince the league to send the Rockets to the Kelowna tournament. And maybe that wouldn't be such a bad thing.

Jacob is an amazing hockey player, Jill thought. *And it would be great to play with him at the tournament.* But she didn't want to be around him if he was going to be angry all the time.

15 Cleaning UP

Logan appeared from around the "boys" SUV. Jacob, his dad and Logan had driven to Kelowna in one vehicle, while Alyssa's mom and the girls took another.

"I can't believe I'm going to clean up garbage in the park when we get back home. I hope this tournament is worth all that," Logan said, stretching and rubbing his eyes.

Jill was surprised he seemed so tired. According to texts from Jacob, Logan had slept the entire four-hour trip from Vancouver to Kelowna. But there he was, looking around as if he'd landed on the moon, not in the Okanagan Valley.

Jill grabbed his hockey bag and dropped it at his feet.

"Whoa, thanks," Logan said. "I could have done that. It's pretty heavy."

"Was it?" said Jill. "I didn't notice. You seemed like you were in distress, so I thought I'd help you."

"Are you making fun of me?"

"I don't know, am I?"

Logan stared at her. The look on his face said he was not sure what was happening. Jill really enjoyed it. She had been trying to challenge the boys on the ice all season. Now she was going to challenge them off it, too. But she didn't want to make a big display of everything. She wanted to show them, not just tell them.

As Logan grabbed his backpack from the back seat, she wondered if he was getting it.

"Picking up garbage isn't that bad," Jill said. "The Blazers have to help, too. And would you rather stay home than come on this trip? We're lucky those letters worked. We should thank Coach Kelly again before the game."

"We've already thanked her ten thousand times," Jacob said, climbing out of the SUV. "But, yeah, I get it. And thank you, Jill and Alyssa, for helping us get here."

Even though he didn't sound that sincere, Jill was happy to hear Jacob say anything positive.

It was late in the afternoon, but the sun was shining. There was no sign of snow or rain. There were mountains in the distance — the top of the valley, Alyssa's dad had said. They were still white, but that was the only lingering sign of winter.

Jacob was standing on the other side of the SUV, helping his dad unload sticks from a rooftop cargo carrier. Jill reached up and offered to grab some, too. He handed her six more.

"I brought extras, just in case," he said.

Jill looked them over. All the sticks looked new. She placed them on the hockey bags and moved to the back of the SUV to pull down the liftgate. It didn't budge.

"It's okay," Jacob said. "I'll get that."

He reached up and pressed a button. The liftgate dropped into place and locked on its own.

Jill wondered if this was how NHL players arrived to play hockey, with six extra sticks and a vehicle that practically drove itself. She looked at her two hockey sticks on her beat-up, old hockey bag. She really hoped she wouldn't have to borrow a stick from Alyssa. She was already hitching a ride with her friend's family and staying in their hotel room.

"One hour until game time," Jacob said. "We play a team from Cranbrook, the Three-on-Three Amigos."

"Cute name," said Alyssa.

"I thought we were in Cranbrook," Logan said.

"Cranbrook is in the Kootenays, way east of here," Jill said. "We're in Kelowna, the Okanagan. You know, the Ogopogo lake monster? Apples and apricots?"

"Don't forget the wine," Mr. Tate said as he sealed up the SUV. "By the way, your mom and I are going wine touring with the other parents. We'll see you after the game."

"Wait, you're not going to watch?" Jacob said.

"Uh, well, I guess not. We'll see the next game. You kids are fine. See ya!"

"Oh, and good luck," Mrs. Tate said.

Jill, Alyssa and the boys grabbed their gear and headed into the rink. It didn't feel like hockey season at all. The air was dry and warmer than Jill was expecting. The rink was not what she was expecting, either. It was a small building in a part of town that seemed to be dedicated to big machinery.

Once they stepped inside, though, she was thrilled. There was just one sheet of ice, and it was just the right size. Like their home rink, it was small enough that it didn't have to be split for three-on-three. Two teams were battling it out when the Rockets arrived at the glass.

"It's a mini-rink," Jacob said. "Cool!"

They scattered to their dressing rooms and changed into their gear in record time.

Coach Kelly called them to the bench to explain some of the rules. "Okay, everyone. Games are twelve-minute periods. There are no offsides, even though there are blue lines. It's mostly the same as at home. And there's one last thing: no fighting."

Logan and Jacob just stared at their skates.

"Boys?"

"It wasn't a fight," Jacob said.

Their coach just gave him a stern look.

"Yes, Coach. No fighting," the boys mumbled.

"Good, enjoy. It looks like a blast. I wish I could play."

Jill scooted to centre ice, drawing groans from her teammates.

"First three at centre!" she shouted.

Dylan and Logan followed. Jill could not believe Jacob just stood there. He was staring around at the rink, as if he was searching for something.

Jill didn't have time to worry about it. The ref blew the whistle, and she found herself at centre ice taking the faceoff.

Oh, no. I've never done this before, she thought.

"Hey, Logan . . ."

Before she could finish her sentence, the ref dropped the puck. She swiped at it and actually managed to bat it between the other player's skates. He was much taller than Jill, and he didn't see where the puck went. Jill saw it first, and she tipped it behind him.

She slipped around him and picked up the puck on the other side of centre. She suddenly had free ice ahead of her. She skated hard straight through the middle of the ice.

The Amigos defender closed down on her with speed. Jill did not have time to think. She simply backhanded a pass to her left.

She was going to charge over to the left wing to retrieve the puck when Logan zoomed into the play. But he didn't keep the puck for long. He sent a pass through the slot to Dylan in the right faceoff circle. Dylan made an easy one-timer into the goal.

"Whoo!" Jill shouted as she skated over to congratulate him.

Logan arrived and the trio tapped one another on the helmet.

"What's gotten into you, girl?" Logan asked. "How did you know I was behind you on the wing?"

"I don't know," Jill said. "I just kind of thought it was the right place to pass."

Jill looked up at the score clock. The Rockets had scored nine seconds into the game. It got the team off to a great start. But the next thing Jill knew, the final buzzer was sounding.

She looked up at the clock again — the only time she had bothered to look since that first goal. She smiled: Rockets 9, Amigos 6.

"How many points did you get?" she asked Logan.

"I dunno, like five or six," he said. "Three goats and three apples, maybe."

"Is that goals and assists?"

"Yeah," he said, turning to Jacob. "Did you get a hat trick, too?"

"I don't remember."

Jill did. As she thought about it, she counted three from Logan plus two from Griffin and one each from Dylan, Lily, Camille and Alyssa — or nine.

Jacob grabbed his extra stick from the corner and skated off the ice without saying anything.

Jill thought he was being childish. Was he really going to pout because he didn't score?

16 In the BOX

The Rockets lost their second game of the tournament against a team from Alberta. Jill was worried the Rockets had lost their confidence, and Jacob seemed to be proof.

"I'm going to sit this one out," Jacob told his teammates as they gathered for their third game. "My ankle is sore again from that injury in the regular season. You guys can beat this team without me, anyway."

"What? No way," Dylan said. "We need you."

"Jacob is important," Jill said. "But we can win this. We only lost 10–6 to that Alberta team, and they were really good. Jacob didn't play much at all that game."

Nobody said anything.

Jill meant it, though, and she wanted her teammates to believe it. "But does it matter?" she added, finally. "Do we really care if we win this? It's like the season. We play the same number of games no matter what. And aren't they all fun?"

Dylan and Logan picked up their gear and went into the dressing room with the other boys.

The girls did the same, but Jill was a bit upset that the boys walked away without saying anything.

Once inside the dressing room, Jill kept talking about what a great time she was having. She was skating better than ever, and she felt even more confident with the puck.

"And, Alyssa," she said, "you're doing amazing. You are even better than during regular hockey, and we're playing with boys."

"Thanks," Alyssa said. "But what is really great is how amazing Teagan is in goal."

Teagan smiled. "Thanks. This is only my second season in goal."

"But the way you played against the Blazers, when they were shooting so hard," Jill marvelled.

"Yeah, some of those shots kind of hurt. But I have all this equipment, so it doesn't hurt much or for long."

The chatter put everyone in a better mood. But the more they talked, the less excited Alyssa seemed to be about the game they were about to play.

Jill was last to finish changing, so she asked Alyssa to wait for her. She wanted to know what was bothering her friend. "You okay?" Jill asked her.

"Yeah, I'm fine."

"Of course you are. I just thought you might be worried about Jacob."

"Nah, he's fine. He's a big boy."

Jill finished taping her socks, doing it slowly so she

could think of something else to say. "Do you know who we are playing?" she said, finally.

"No, I always leave that to Jacob," Alyssa said. "But you know, don't you?"

Jill was a bit surprised. She had not expected that.

"I guess I'm being kind of obvious," Jill said.

"Kind of. Why are you so worried? I didn't think you really liked my brother."

"No, it's not that at all. I just don't get why he seems so angry. I don't remember him being like that before."

Alyssa's face changed. She leaned against the wall of the dressing room. Jill was sure she was going to cry.

"I know," Alyssa said. "He says mean stuff all the time. He's always getting into trouble at home. My parents almost didn't let him come here. And not just because of the fight. He's not doing well in school."

Jill was sorry for asking so many questions. She hadn't known it was that bad, and she didn't know what to say.

"We're playing the Grape Apes," said Jill, trying to get Alyssa to smile. "They're from Kelowna. You know, grapes and wine?"

"That's cute," Alyssa said. She was crying a little.

"You worried about Jacob?"

"Yeah. My dad said he's 'throwing away a chance of a lifetime,'" she said, making air quotes with her fingers. "Mom said we are all being too hard on him, and if he quits, he quits. It's his choice."

Jill wasn't sure what to say. "I would give a million dollars to be able to play hockey like your brother. He's so much fun to watch." She thought about the time Jacob had surprised her. "And he passes to us. That girl on the Blazers said the boys never pass to their girls." Jill sighed. "I wish I could help you. You're both my friends."

Alyssa stopped crying and smiled.

Jill could hear the noise as they walked from the dressing room to the ice. The arena was full, and Jill could see the other team had plenty of fans. The crowd was cheering loudly. Some had signs, and some were banging pots or ringing bells.

Jill was suddenly more nervous than she had been in a long time. But she was as excited as she was nervous. She looked into the crowd, and the fans were all smiling and waving at them. There were little girls in the crowd, too.

Jill felt good about that until the game started.

In the first ten minutes, she was called for tripping and interference. She almost never got penalties. But now she had two in ten minutes.

Jill was mumbling to herself on the bench. Jacob came over from where he had been standing with the coach.

"Hey, tough girl, take it easy on the other team." He was clearly joking, and it did make Jill laugh.

By the time she was ready for her next shift, Jill had forgotten about the penalties. She grabbed a loose puck on the right wing. Instead of skating at the net, she curled back to centre ice.

Dylan was drifting toward his own goal on defence. It opened up the entire middle of the ice. Jill and Logan made eye contact, and she backhanded a pass into empty space.

Logan raced from the left wing into the centre to get the puck. Dylan followed and took his place along the left. Jill settled into the defensive position.

The boys passed quickly back and forth. Suddenly, Logan snapped a goal into the top of the net.

It was amazing to watch. The crowd went quiet.

The Grape Apes were not very good. The Rockets were ahead 5–1 in the first period, even after Jill's penalties. Jill felt bad for them, and their fans.

"We should go easy on them," she said on the bench. "What happens if we keep scoring?"

"We win," Dylan said.

Jill didn't think that was a very good answer. She wasn't sure what to do next, but it was her turn on the ice. She jumped through the gate without looking and crashed into a girl from the other team.

The referee raised his hand again. "Two minutes, interference," she said.

Jill stopped skating and looked at the ref, then to her bench. Everyone on the Rockets was laughing.

"Hey, Jill, is this how you plan to make it easier for them?" Jacob shouted.

Jill slowly skated to the penalty box. Three penalties in one game. She couldn't believe it.

To make matters worse, the Grape Apes scored, and suddenly their fans were cheering louder than ever.

17 Grape JAM

Jill looked up at the scoreboard: Rockets 6, Grape Apes 4. There were just six minutes left in the game, and the fans were going wild. Jill thought of how she felt when they were quiet. She missed it.

Coach Kelly called the players over to the bench during a break. Jill had a hard time hearing her over the noise of the crowd. The arena was small, and it meant the Grape Apes fans were all around them.

"You're still ahead by two," Coach Kelly shouted. "Don't worry about the other team. Play your game."

It was all she bothered to say. Jill tried to take it to heart, but the coach was smiling widely. Jill did not think she was really that worried about the wins or losses. Coach looked like she was having a great time.

Jill, in contrast, was a nervous wreck. If they won this game, they would play in the championship semifinal and avoid the consolation bracket. Jill hadn't said anything because she knew the Grape Apes were in last place. She had been sure the Rockets would have no trouble winning.

She had also told her team that winning didn't matter. But she had to admit to herself she wanted to win.

She shuffled down the bench to get ready for her next shift. Just as she got to the door, the crowd exploded again. The Rockets were only one goal ahead.

"They need a girl goal now," Jacob coached from the bench. "That will slow them down. Jill, you and Logan should play together. Dylan should stay on defence. Guys, set up Jill. We'll win for sure."

The trio took to the ice. They had been trying the same kind of play almost the whole tournament, and Jill was certain the other team had started to catch on to their move. Jill would skate down the right wing. The centre would skate into the middle of the ice. The defence would pass it, and the centre would deflect it to Jill's side. She would have a head start, and usually got to the puck first. Then she'd pass in front, where one of the boys was waiting.

Dylan tapped his stick and called Jill's name as they prepared for the faceoff.

"Switch," he said.

Jill was suddenly nervous. Dylan wanted her to play defence so she could be in a position to score. She skated slowly, leaning over a little, to trade spots with Dylan. He skated toward her and nudged her out of his way.

"Hey, winning doesn't matter, right? We play the same number of games, right? So get back there and score a goal."

Jill wasn't sure his pep talk was working. Logan was a great centre, and he almost always won his faceoffs. Jill would have to take the puck and skate around until he was open for the pass.

She gripped her stick and crouched into a ready position. Sure enough, Logan won the faceoff, but the puck got stuck in his skates. There was a battle for it at centre, and Jill could see the puck was just sitting there.

She had no idea what to do, so she stopped thinking. She zoomed forward and fished the puck from the tangled skates. Now she was out of position. She was too close to Logan, and she needed to retreat into her own end.

She skated backwards as hard as she could with the puck. The other team spotted her and began to skate toward her.

Jill panicked and threw the puck up the ice. Now she was stuck on defence for good, and the other team had the puck.

Logan and Dylan moved ahead to forecheck as the other team set up a breakout. Jill stayed in position near centre ice, hoping the boys would stop them.

But the Grape Apes were really pushing to tie the game. The player behind their goal faked left and skated right. He passed it to his centre, and they cleared their blue line.

Now they were skating up the ice as a unit. Jill backpedalled as best she could.

Dylan was to Jill's left. He poked at the puck. It must have worked to make the Grape Apes player nervous, because he passed to the girl in the centre.

The boys kept close to their wingers, and the girl from the Grape Apes skated up the middle toward Jill. Jill was still trying to skate backwards to make sure she did not give up a breakaway. But she could feel herself backing closer to Teagan in the goal.

Jill needed to do something. She thought about moving over slightly in hopes the girl would take a shot.

But that would probably end with a faceoff in their end. Or worse, a Grape Apes goal. Instead, Jill stopped suddenly and poke-checked the other player.

The puck squirted in the other direction and Logan swooped in to grab it. He dumped it back around the Rockets' net, where Jill retreated to collect it.

Now Jill was leading the breakout. She felt better about the other team not having the puck. But she was nervous about starting the play. The boys looped back toward her, but she did not pass to them. She had to skate it out herself for the play to work.

She glanced up at the clock: four minutes to play. The girl on the other team was not being aggressive. Maybe she figured that Jill wouldn't try to score, since the Rockets didn't need a girl goal. The Grape Apes player was hanging back in the high slot in front of Teagan.

It gave Jill a bit of room, but she would have to be quick.

She came out slowly from behind the net on Teagan's left side. Jill was sure if the defender came at her, she could make a wide circle around her. But the defender didn't move. She was just sitting in the middle, clogging up the passing lane.

Jill had to get her to move. She lifted her stick and faked a slap pass.

Nope, nothing.

Jill wanted to get the play going. The boys were still doing laps up and down their wings. She couldn't wait any longer. She put her head down and started to skate for her blue line. The other girl tried to skate backwards, but Jill was going too fast. Jill reached her blue line and Logan skated toward her, banging his stick. Dylan took off down the right side.

Jill suddenly had an idea.

She lifted her stick again, only this time hit the puck as hard as she could. It skipped past Logan all the way to the other end of the ice where it banged off the end boards.

Dylan was skating with all the power he had. Jill did the same. She needed to get to the far post. She was pounding away on her skates, not even looking at where she was going.

She crossed the other team's blue line and peeked ahead of her. Dylan had the puck, but she was still too far back from the net. She drifted into the centre and he floated a pass.

Jill hardly had any time to aim. But there! She thought she saw room above the goalie's blocker.

She watched the puck come to her stick and smacked it with all her strength.

Everything seemed to be in slow motion. Jill watched the puck race to the net. But it wasn't in the air. She had not hit it properly. It was scooting along the ice.

No, Jill thought. *It's not even close.*

18 Three's a CROWD

The puck went in.

Jill couldn't believe it. It couldn't be true! But the referee was pointing to the net. Her teammates were celebrating.

The crowd was silent.

"Did I score?" she asked as Dylan and Logan tapped her on the helmet.

"Well, I didn't," Dylan said.

"How?"

"You hit the puck, it went between the goalie's legs. It's really simple."

Jill finally cracked a smile. She was happy to look at the scoreboard now: Rockets 7, Apes 5. There were only seconds to play, and the clock was still ticking down to zero.

Jill let out a sigh of relief as she finally reached the bench. Jacob shuffled over to her behind the bench and smacked her shoulder pads.

"Nice whiff," he said.

"Huh?"

"You had such a big windup, the goalie nearly jumped out of her skates. She played the top corner and opened the five-hole. The puck slid right through along the ice. It was genius."

"Just how I planned it." They didn't need to know the puck went in by accident.

Jill couldn't stop smiling as the game ended. She gathered the team in the hallway outside the dressing room and told them the good news: they'd be playing in the championship semifinal the next morning.

"And I'm sure Jacob will be good to play," she said.

He nodded, and they went into their dressing rooms to change.

★★★

The next time Jill and Alyssa saw their teammates was half an hour later in the outdoor pool at the hotel. Jill could not remember a time she needed to dunk herself so badly. The three games in one day were bad enough. But playing three games of three-on-three was gruelling. She had to peel her equipment off her body.

Every muscle was sore, and her mind was spinning. She sat on the side of the pool and dangled her feet in the water until she felt better.

"Who do we play tomorrow?" Jacob asked as he walked over to her. He sat next to Jill on the steps of the ladder to the deep end.

"The winner of the B pool," she said. "They're from the United States. I think they're called the Hawks."

"That name's kind of boring. I thought everyone had cool team names."

"Yeah, me, too. How's your ankle?"

"Meh, it's fine. I probably could have played. But Coach Kelly suggested I take it easy."

Jacob started to climb down the ladder, deeper into the pool. Jill wanted him to know she knew he was nervous about the WHL draft. But she didn't want to make him mad by mentioning it.

"So have you decided about the academy?"

Jacob froze on the ladder. "How'd you know about that?"

"Your sister told me. You know, she's really worried about you."

"She is? I doubt it. She doesn't care about me."

Jill was shocked. That was not what she saw in the change room before the last game. "She's your twin sister, Jacob. How could she not care about you? She told me how much she was worrying just before the game."

Just as Jill said that, they heard someone yelling. They looked up in time to see Alyssa jumping into the pool. Her cannonball showered them with water.

Jill waited for Alyssa to resurface so she could get some revenge. But Alyssa stayed underwater. They could see her hanging out near the bottom.

"She can really hold her breath," Jill said.

"She's hiding because she knows I'm going to get her back," Jacob added.

It felt like a minute had passed, and Alyssa was in the same spot. Jill suddenly felt sick.

Jacob climbed higher to get a better look. Jill looked at him, and he looked scared.

"Is she okay?" Jill asked, worried.

Jacob dove into the deep end. Jill watched as he swam to his sister. They both emerged from the bottom, sputtering and shouting.

"Let me go!" Alyssa said.

"We thought you were drowning!" Jacob yelled.

They splashed water at each other. Jacob swam away and Alyssa grabbed the side of the pool.

"I was just joking!" she yelled at him.

"Stupid joke!"

Jill tried to give her friend the "I'm disappointed, but I'm not going to yell" look her mom was so good at giving her. "He's right. You totally freaked us out."

Alyssa had a silly smile on her face. "Thank you for trying to save me," she shouted as her brother went into the hot tub.

"Next time you won't be so lucky," he grumped. "And stop telling people my secrets."

Now it was Alyssa's turn to get grumpy. She pulled herself from the water onto the pool deck next to Jill. "What did you say to him?"

"I'm sorry," said Jill. "It just kind of spilled out. I wanted him to know we're worried about him. That we're on his side."

"I should have never told you. He's my brother. Why are you getting involved, anyway?"

"You're both my friends. Sorry if I made you mad."

"Whatever. You're not captain off the ice, you know."

"I'm not captain of this team at all. I didn't want to get involved. I just got sick of the roller-coaster ride with your brother."

The sun was down, suddenly. Jill stood to get her towel from the chair behind her. She stood on the pool deck and looked out over Okanagan Lake and the hills behind it. She looked back at Alyssa, who was looking the other way from the edge of the pool.

A wind picked up, and Jill decided she wanted to warm up. She walked over to the hot tub and sat on the steps.

"I'm sorry," she said to Jacob.

"Whatever," he said. "It doesn't matter."

Only the bubbling jets broke the silence until Alyssa stood. She grabbed her towel and walked past them both.

"You wouldn't even be here if it wasn't for us," she said over her shoulder as she left the pool deck.

Jill felt her cheeks get red and warm with embarrassment.

Did she mean I wouldn't be here without their car and them paying for the hotel? Jill wondered.

Did Alyssa really see Jill as a burden? Jill wondered if she should call her parents. Or take a bus home, if that was even possible. She felt stuck and alone.

19 Semifinal SUNDAY

Jill sat alone in the hotel lobby. It was an hour before their semifinal.

She watched as Alyssa and her mom came out of the elevator. The girls had not said two words to each other all night, even though they shared a room with Alyssa's mom.

Jill watched as Alyssa and her mom went to the buffet table for breakfast.

Jill had woken up early and eaten with some other players. She felt in her pocket for the $20 her mom had given her "just in case." She had planned to give it to Alyssa's parents. She would say thank you and that she wanted to ride home with someone else. Jill was still trying to figure out what to do about the car ride home. She thought about asking Teagan or Lily if there was room with them.

But she lost her nerve. Instead, she smiled and followed Alyssa and her mom to their car once they had finished eating. If Alyssa's mom knew what was going on, she didn't say anything. Or maybe the whole family was sick of her.

It was another quiet car ride, and another quiet trip into the dressing room. Jill watched as everyone arrived to put on their equipment. They all looked tired and worn out.

Jill stumbled from the dressing room onto the ice. She skated a few lazy laps as warm-up. She was not thinking about the game at all. She barely remembered who they were playing. All Jill could remember was the team was from Spokane, Washington. They had a hawk logo on their jerseys.

Jill felt like she was in a daze the first two periods. She barely touched the puck. She barely said anything to anyone.

As the puck dropped to start the third period, Jill sat alone at the end of the bench. She undid her helmet straps, lifted her cage and grabbed a towel from the bench to wipe her face.

It wasn't so much to get the sweat from her eyes as to try to wake herself up. She tossed the towel back, reconnected her helmet with two hard snaps and looked around. Everyone looked tired. It had been a long weekend.

There wasn't much chatter on the bench and the stands were nearly empty. Jill caught a glimpse of the scoreboard. Somehow, the Rockets were leading 4–3.

She could barely remember who had scored. It was nearly her turn for a shift when something startled her.

She looked up just in time to see a puck roll around to the front of the Rockets bench. Logan raced to it, then stopped suddenly, throwing snow up into Jill's face.

"Whoa!" Jill said.

She had never seen Logan skate that hard before. He rimmed the puck back along the boards to the other side. Jacob was there to pick it up, but he didn't keep it.

Jacob hit a hard slap pass back to Logan, who had moved into the zone. Logan had found some open space, and was alone when the pass arrived. He just kept his stick on the ice. The puck banked off his blade and into the net.

"Yeah!" Jill shouted as she jumped to her feet.

She had not seen the boys play like that before. She banged her stick on the boards to celebrate.

The passing play seemed to wake her up. She had some jump when she finally got onto the ice. Jacob stayed on the ice to finish his shift, and Jill stepped through the gate with Dylan.

Jill watched as Jacob won the faceoff and the puck skidded toward her. She chipped it ahead past her defender and skated into the zone. She decided to try what Logan had done, and hit it hard along the boards. It felt funny. There was no one on the other side to get the pass.

The Spokane goalie came out of her net to trap the puck, but it skipped over her stick and dribbled into the far corner.

Dylan was first to it. He was flying. He won the battle along the boards and looked up. Jill faked like she was going to the net. Then she changed directions and went into the slot. Dylan floated a pass to her and, just as it reached her, she caught sight of something from the corner of her eye.

She was sure it was Jacob. Jill didn't keep the pass long. As fast as she could, she settled the puck and sent it to where she thought Jacob might be waiting.

It worked. Jacob had a step on his defender and picked up the pass along the right wing. Jill watched as he took a wrist shot from close to the goal. He was nearly behind the net, but flipped the puck high. Jill had no idea how Jacob could hit the crossbar and get the puck into the net from where he was standing. The other team's goalie was playing really close to her posts, but Jacob still scored.

"Yeah!" Jill shouted.

The Rockets led 6–3.

"That'll show 'em what they missed," Dylan said as the trio celebrated.

Jill was confused. Who missed what? As the Rockets continued to score, the only thing she could think of was that the boys were trying to prove something. But what?

At least the team was playing better than Jill had ever seen. They beat the Hawks 8–5. They were going to the final.

20 Last CHANCE

Jill could hardly believe they were in the tournament final. A few days before, they had been begging for forgiveness from their league. Now they were playing a team that looked really amazing in warm-ups. She caught a glimpse of a jersey: Saskatoon Wildcats.

Huh, Jill thought. *They look intense. This could be tough.*

She was stretching at centre ice when one of the Wildcats plopped down near her.

"Hey," he said. "Is your team from Alberta?"

Jill looked up at the boy. He was smiling at her.

She smiled back. "Oh, ah, no. We're from Vancouver."

"Canucks fans, eh? We all cheer for the Oilers. We watched your semifinal. Who is number 18?"

Jill looked around at her team. She had to think of the numbers. "Oh, that's Jacob."

"He's good. Was he drafted?"

"Jacob? He was accepted at a hockey academy."

"No, no. I meant was he drafted yesterday in the WHL draft?"

"I don't think so."

"Really? Huh, that's weird. He's pretty awesome. Our boy Vince went in the ninth round." He pointed to one of his teammates who was flipping the puck into the air and catching it on his blade. "Anyway, good luck. I'm Paul, by the way."

"Oh, hi. I'm Jill."

Paul skated back to his team. Jill went back to stretching. But she couldn't help thinking about what Paul had said about the draft. Why didn't Jacob or Alyssa say anything? Then she realized it: Jacob hadn't been drafted. That's why Alyssa was so angry.

She skated up to Alyssa. "Hey, look . . ."

"It's okay," Alyssa interrupted her. "I know my brother and I have been hard to be with this weekend. I'm sorry if you feel stuck with us. You didn't say much yesterday."

"No, not at all, I love you guys," Jill said. "I thought you were sick of me always tagging along. You said at the pool that I wouldn't be here without you."

"Oh, Jilly Bean, I wasn't talking to you then," Alyssa said. "I meant that for my brother. None of the boys would be here if it wasn't for us."

Jill thought it out. The comment made as much sense about Jacob as it did about her. She felt relieved, and a little silly for thinking that her best friend would resent her.

Jill felt much better as the game started, and her

good mood got even better right away. The Saskatoon players were joking and laughing with each other and the Rockets. They were even joking with the referees.

Paul skated past their bench, took a pass and stopped. He flipped his stick upside down so the blade was under his arm. He tried to pass the puck with the handle of his hockey stick.

It hardly went anywhere.

"That's three points for me. It went forward!"

Logan wooshed in and grabbed the puck away from Paul, who was using his hockey stick like a cane now. Logan was laughing so hard he didn't get very far with the puck and the Wildcats won the puck back from him.

Jill didn't think she had ever laughed that much in a game. It went back and forth, but with almost no goals. By the time the second water break came, the game was 3–3.

Paul leaned over on the Rockets bench with his water bottle.

"We can't score without making five passes first," Paul said. "That's really hard."

"Why? Don't you want to win?" Jacob asked him.

"I can't even believe we are in the finals," Paul said. "The only reason we're winning is because we have Vince. Every time he shoots, it goes in the net. We didn't come here to win. This is just a big weekend for our parents. We decided we would all play different positions. And you get points for different things, like flipping your stick over or shooting with the wrong hand."

"What do you win, for the points?" Wade asked.

"Oh, I dunno," Paul said. "We didn't get that far."

The ref blew his whistle and the players got into position for the final period. Jill jumped through the gate.

The ref dropped the puck. Jacob won it straight back to Logan, who carried it hard up the right wing.

In two big strides, Vince crossed over to that side, skating backwards. He swatted the puck off Logan's stick, changed direction and picked up the loose puck on his stick.

Jill had never seen anything happen so quickly.

Paul skated back into his own zone. He passed back and forth with Vince really quickly.

"One, two, three, four," Paul shouted. "One more pass."

A girl on the Wildcats skated past Jill. "Open!" she shouted.

"Tracey's open!" Paul shouted.

He looked up, but he didn't pass to her.

"Nope, Jill is there. She's going to steal the puck!"

Jacob pressured him, and Paul lost the puck.

"Now we gotta start over!" Paul shouted again.

Jacob did finally score — banging in a rebound from in close. But Vince scored for Saskatoon when he deflected a point shot at the side of the net.

The buzzer sounded, and it was 4–4.

The ref skated to the benches. "No time for overtime," he said. "Penalty shots. Three shooters each."

The players all gasped with excitement.

"Oh, can I shoot?" Lily asked.

"Anyone else?" Coach Kelly asked.

Everyone put up their hands. Everyone but Jill.

She had never taken a penalty shot. She was not sure if she could even skate, she was so nervous just thinking about it.

21 SHOOTOUT

Paul shouted over to the Rockets. "We're sending three girls. Girls get two points for every shootout goal."

"Is that true?" Jacob asked. "We could win this. All we have to do is send two girls and I'll shoot."

Jill couldn't let that happen. "No, it's a challenge. We should send three girls, too."

"Yeah!" Lily said. "Me, Alyssa and who else?"

All the girls cheered. All the boys groaned.

"Too late, we decided," Jill said, suddenly excited by the idea.

"Okay, Jill will shoot third," Lily said.

"No, wait!" Jill said. "I can't . . . I mean I'm not great at shootouts. Macy should go, she's a great shooter."

"If you're sure, then Macy can go."

The boys were shifting uncomfortably on the bench. "You gotta send your best shooter second," Jacob said.

"Oh, thanks, brother," Alyssa said. "But we have our strategy."

The Wildcats won the toss and shot first, but their girl missed wide.

Everyone on the Wildcats tapped their sticks on the ice as Alyssa skated to centre. She skated slowly with the puck toward the goal. She faked a shot so the goalie moved and then scored a wrist shot into the top corner.

"Whoa!" Jacob shouted. "I totally taught her that move."

The second Wildcats girl also missed, this time hitting Teagan right in the chest for an easy save.

"Whoo, Teags!" Jill shouted.

Lily was next. She tried to deke, but her backhand didn't get the puck into the air. It hit the goalie's leg pad.

"Tracey!" Paul shouted from his bench.

The Wildcats forward picked up the puck at centre and drifted to the right-wing boards. She skated at the near post like she was going to backhand it on the short side. But, instead, she pulled it to her forehand — and scored!

That was amazing, Jill thought.

It was Macy's turn, and she took a short spin near the boards and took a big breath.

"No pressure," Logan said. "But if you score, we win."

"I actually didn't know that until just now," Macy said, her voice filled with sarcasm. "Thanks, Logan."

Jill's heart was pounding in her chest as Macy took her position.

Macy skated in from the wing and tried to fake. But the puck rolled off her stick. She pulled it back just in time, but now she was almost at the goal. The only thing Macy could do was try a backhand. She tried to flip it high, but it just dribbled past the goal.

It was still tied after three shooters.

"We have, like, a twelve-hour drive home," Paul called over to the Rockets. "So let's settle this. Send your best!"

Everyone on the Rockets watched as the Wildcats sent their fourth shooter — another girl.

"She's their best?" Wade asked. "What about that Vince?"

The Wildcats player tried to shoot for the top corner, but Teagan snatched it from the air.

"Yes!" Jill screamed.

"Send Jacob," Dylan said.

"I agree," said Logan.

"No way!" Jill shouted. Every girl on the team shouted the same thing with her.

"Never going to happen," Alyssa said. "You guys got enough time on the ice this weekend. 'Let the girls play the girls.' Isn't that what you told the Blazers, Jake? We never needed you to protect us.

But you could stand up for us now. The way the Wildcats are doing for their girl teammates."

Jacob didn't say anything.

"That's what I thought," Alyssa said. "Now, Jill, you should score and let everyone go home."

Jill snapped her head to look at Alyssa. "Me? Why?"

"Because you're the one who got us here," Macy said.

"Jill has been working hardest on her skills," Lily added.

Jill couldn't believe it. Her teammates were all nodding their heads in agreement.

"Just shoot for her five-hole," Teagan said. "I've been watching."

"Good advice," Jacob added. "Goalies always know other goalies."

Jill nodded and moved to centre. From the Wildcats bench, Paul started chanting "Jill, Jill, Jill!" and everyone laughed. It actually made Jill feel better. She felt like she was just playing hockey with her friends, not taking a shootout goal to win a tournament.

She skated from centre with the puck, wondering how she was going to deke. She crossed into the high slot and looked up at their goalie. That's when Jill spotted it, a huge space between the goalie's skates.

Jill lunged forward and smacked the puck as quickly and with as much force as she could muster. It zipped through the air just off the ice. It thumped off the inside of the goalie's leg pad and into the net.

"Goal!" the referee shouted.

Jill hit the brakes and turned. She watched as all her teammates poured off the bench toward her to swarm her with hugs and high-fives.

She laughed as they each tapped her helmet. Alyssa and Jacob were last to get to her.

Jill didn't know what to say, but she knew what she had to do. She gave her best friend a hug. Jacob grabbed them both.

Jill looked around the tiny arena. All the parents were standing and clapping.

The Rockets formed a line to shake hands with the Wildcats.

"Hey, nice job," Paul said.

"Thanks," Jill said. "That was the most fun I've ever had. Your team was awesome."

Down the line, Vince was shaking Jacob's hand. "Good game, man. Maybe we'll play against each other in Junior in a couple of years."

"Oh, Jacob is quitting hockey," Alyssa told him. "He's doing parkour."

"That would be too bad. But whatever makes you happy," Vince said. "We've gotta get in that car. Only twelve hours to get home!"

"Safe trip," Alyssa said as the Wildcats left the ice.

"Do you think that guy was serious?" Jacob asked Jill and his sister. "About playing Junior."

"Yeah, I think he was," Jill said. "Parkour is cool,

but you're a pretty amazing hockey player. You should think about sticking with it."

"Yeah, maybe," he said.

"Hey, and if you need help, we'll stand up for you," Alyssa said, smiling.

"Are you sure?" Jacob asked. "Going by the Bambi Brawl video, Jill has a hard time standing up on her own." He ducked the glove Jill threw at his head.

"Parkour, hockey — whatever makes you happy, Jacob," Jill repeated Vince's words. "As for three-on-three, I think I've got it from here."

ACKNOWLEDGEMENTS

None of my books would have been possible without the guidance, assistance and insights of my editor, Kat Mototsune. However, it bears repeating here because Kat was instrumental in carrying this book through to completion. She went above and beyond. Thank you Kat, and thank you once again to the staff at Lorimer who always elevate and present the material with utmost professionalism. Finally, this book is dedicated to all athletes — male or female — who have overcome their fears to achieve something special.